Daddy Dom 4

Mountain Daddy Does it Better

+

James's Baby Girls

A DDLG and ABDL 2 in 1 novel collection

of kinky BDSM age play stories

By Tina Moore

Table of Contents

Mountain Daddy Does it Better

A Romantic Novel About a Daddy Dom who Trains His Baby Girl in the DDLG and ABDL kink

By Tina Moore

Chapter 1

Lana's hybrid skidded wildly in the mud as she gripped the wheel so hard that her knuckles turned white, forcefully guiding the sedan back onto the road. According to the map, she was only twenty minutes away from the cabin which she had rented for the summer in a secluded spot in the Georgia mountains. If the rain kept up like it was, then it was going to be a whole lot longer before she was finally out of this car.

She had driven straight here from Orlando, Florida, opting to travel in one long marathon session rather than breaking it up into two shorter trips. It was a long, boring drive through mostly farmland but everything was going as planned until this thunderstorm came seemingly out of nowhere. As she squinted through the dark, trying desperately to stay on the road, she was beginning to wonder if that had been a bad plan. Of course, originally the plan had involved a tag-team effort.

She wasn't supposed to be taking this trip alone. Her boyfriend Mike had convinced her that they should take advantage of the two-month vacation that came with being an office lady at a local school by renting a cabin and escaping the heat and humidity of the Florida summer. He was a writer, after all, and could work from anywhere, he had argued. He had painted a lovely picture of the two of them tucked away in their little love nest in the mountains, far away from the problems of real life. Lana agreed, eager for a change in scenery, and booked the cabin. The entire trip was on her credit card, of course. He was always suggesting things to do and then asking her to pay for them, saying that writing didn't pay very well, as if teaching were some lucrative career that kept her rolling in money.

Then, only a week before they were supposed to leave, he dumped her out of the blue. He said that he had met a model who was in town from Miami and that they were in love and were going to move in together. Lana had cried so many tears over that man, and she was sure she would cry many more. Her instinct had been to pay the cancellation fee and stay home to tend to her broken heart, but her friend Barb had convinced her that a change in scenery would do her good.

"Forget about that cheating bastard for a few weeks. See if you can find a handsome, rugged mountain man to take your mind off things," she had said. Lana had blushed at that last suggestion but had to admit that the idea had merit. Why should she sit around feeling sorry for herself while he was off with having the time of his life? She should look at this as dodging a bullet. Better to find out now that Mike was disloyal rather than years down the road. She wiped a tear from her eye.

Lana's car started picking up speed as she went down a sharp incline. She tapped her brakes, but the mud was too slippery. She was going too fast when she saw the downed branch, and it was too late to avoid it. It clattered underneath the car, tangling itself in the tires. She slid into the ditch, and that was the last thing she remembered for a long time.

***

Micah's oversized tires were having some trouble getting through the mud. It took a really bad storm to bog down his truck, and this one was a real doozy. With a muttered curse, he had pretty much decided to head back to his hunting cabin, unwilling to fight this chaos just for some beer. Just then, he saw headlights off in the bushes. His heart leaped into his throat at the thought of someone hurt or worse, and he brought his truck to a stop, shifting it into park and putting on his hazards. He hadn't thought to bring an umbrella, it had hardly been sprinkling when he left, and he was soaked immediately upon stepping out onto the muddy dirt road.

He went slowly, cautiously toward the crashed

vehicle, hoping it wouldn't be something beyond his limited ability to help. An ambulance would have a hell of a time getting up here in these conditions. With a shaky hand, he pushed some branches aside and pulled the driver's side door open. It was dented, but it still opened without too much of a fight. Hunched over the steering wheel was a young woman with dark hair. He couldn't tell much else about her, including her health status.

"Ma'am," he said softly, not wanting to startle her. "Are you ok?" There was no response at first, so he nudged her arm gently. She groaned at that, and he sighed in relief. At least she was alive.

"Ma'am, can you move?" She groaned again and shifted her head. She wasn't totally awake yet, but she seemed to be coming around a little. "We need to get you to a doctor. I'm going to help you out of the car now. We can take my truck into town." Her eyes fluttered open, but she couldn't seem to be able to focus on anything, and they quickly closed again. He put his arm gingerly around her waist, worried about overstepping his bounds or injuring her further.

"Let me know if I hurt you, ma'am," he said as he slid his arms underneath her small frame and began to lift her out. She didn't make any noises, only wrapped her arms around his neck, tight as anything.

She's a strong little thing, he thought. *That's a good sign.* He held her close to him, trying to shield her from the rain as much as possible as he carried her to the passenger side of his truck, laying her on the front seat as gently as he could. As he came around to the driver's side, he got a better look at the spot where she had skidded off the road. It was going to be a challenge making it over the deep ruts her spinning tires had made in the road, but it was doable. He got in, grateful to be out of the deluge once again.

"Are you ok, little one?" he muttered, not really expecting a response from the unconscious woman. He put his hand on her forehead, brushing away the wet hair that was stuck to her skin. By the light of the dashboard, he could tell that she was pretty, brownish hair and delicate features. She seemed tiny compared to him, and her petite frame was shivering from head to toe. He cranked up the heat, cursing himself for not having a blanket or spare jacket in the truck. But how could he have known? It was the middle of May, after all.

"Don't worry," he said, putting the truck into drive. "We'll have you fixed up in no time at all." Despite his false optimism, it was slow going. The roads seemed to be getting worse by the minute. He had only made it a little more than half a mile when he heard the local radio station announce that the main road into town was washed out due to a mudslide and that several other roads into town were being closed as well as a precautionary measure. All residents were advised to stay in their homes until further notice. Micah looked at the little bundle on the seat next to him, his heart sinking more and more by the second. He knew his way around a first aid kit well enough, but she needed more than that. Under the circumstances, however, it might be a while before she could get the care she needed. He hated feeling so helpless. His protective instincts were in overdrive, but he didn't have many options. For the moment, the only thing he could do was to take her somewhere warm and comfortable and call a doctor for advice, then wait for the roads to clear. He slapped the steering wheel, frustrated as hell. After a moment of fuming, he put the truck into reverse and made his way back to his hunting cabin. There was nothing for it. He would just have to take care of her by himself.

Chapter 2

When Lana woke up, she stretched her arms and yawned before suddenly freezing. The last thing she remembered, she had been driving in the rain. How did she get to this comfortable, dry place? She opened her eyes to see that she was on a small bed, covered by a thick blanket. It was a small room that was sparsely decorated. Her hair was damp, as were her clothes.

"Hello?" she called out, feeling disoriented and more than a little dizzy. "Anyone home?" A man hurriedly came into the room, a huge mountain of a man, and waved awkwardly at her from the doorway. He didn't look familiar to her, and she squinted at him, more confused than ever.

"Hello, ma'am," he said. "Sorry to just whisk you away like that. You were hurt, and I couldn't just leave you. Do you remember crashing your car?" She shook her head, but just as she did, the memories came flooding back to her. The branch in the road, the screech of metal on wood, the sudden pain. "Oh, yeah," she said vaguely, then lay back down on the pillow. "It was raining."

"Right. It's still raining, and the roads are washed out. I called the hospital and told them what happened. They said the best thing for you right now is rest. Are you hurt, are you in any pain?" She did a careful scan of her body, noticing for the first time a throbbing ache in her wrist.

"My wrist hurts," she said through parched lips. "And I'm dizzy. And thirsty." His brow wrinkled, and she noticed that once you got past his size, he was a very handsome man. He had black hair, beautiful sea-green eyes, and a chiseled jawline. He seemed a few years older than her, early thirties perhaps. His frame was both tall and broad, but his form seemed toned, well-muscled. Even in her compromised position, she couldn't help but notice that he was wearing the hell out of those blue jeans.

"Wait right here," he said. "I'll get you water and an ice pack." He was gone for several minutes, the sound of running water coming from the next room. It occurred to her that he could be a psychopath and that she could be trapped in some kind of reverse Misery scenario. However, as he came back into the room with a pink sippy cup in one hand and a bag of frozen peas in the other, it did seem rather unlikely. Even if it were the case, she was in very little position to do anything about it. He put the peas on the bedside table and brought the sippy cup over to the bed. Lana tried to sit up to drink, but he stopped her.

"The doctor said to rest, so that's what you're going to do, little one." He put his giant paw of a hand under her head and lifted it so that she could drink. "All of it," he prompted when she tried to lay her head back down again. His voice was firm and authoritative, and Lana could feel herself responding to his dominant energy. It put her at ease but also excited her in a way that caught her off guard. She drank all the water down and licked her lips with a satisfied sigh as her body soaked in the hydration. Already, she felt a little more energetic and a little more alert. He picked up the peas and held them against her swollen wrist. She winced at the pressure but was grateful to feel the coolness against her fevered flesh. Hopefully, it would numb the pain entirely after a while.

"Who are you?" she asked and then blushed. "Sorry if that sounded rude. I meant, what is your name?" He chuckled and nodded.

"Not rude at all, ma'am. I reckon you have a right to ask as many questions as you would like. My name is Micah, and this is my hunting cabin. I like to come here a couple of times a year, you know, get away from it all. I was going to make a quick beer run when all hell let loose. I saw you in the ditch and tried to get you to the hospital, but it was already too late, the mudslide had already blocked the roads. I'm afraid we're stuck here until morning at least. Where were you headed? Is there someone I can call?" She shook her head and instantly regretted it as the world began to spin even faster. Maybe it would be better to use her words.

"There's no one to call, just some friends back home. I'm here on vacation. The agent was going to leave the key in a dropbox for me since I was coming into town so late," she said.

"Oh, ok. So you're here alone, then?" She sighed and bit her lip before answering.

"Yes, I was supposed to be coming here with my boyfriend but, well," She trailed off, looking very sad.

"But you guys are no longer together," he guessed, nodding sympathetically. "I've been there. What about your family?"

"My Mom passed a few years back, and I never met my Dad. No siblings. It was just my Mom and I, and now it's just me."

"Oh boy, I just keep asking all the wrong questions, don't I? I promise I'm not trying to make you relive these terrible things on purpose." Lana got a wry chuckle out of that.

"It's not your fault that I'm having an

unlucky streak lately. Don't worry about it," she replied. He scratched his head and looked abashed. It was a good look on him.

"Well, anyway, the doc said you should rest. Hold tight for just a second, Lana." He grabbed the sippy cup and went back to the kitchen to refill it, rifling around in the cabinets before returning. In his comfortingly oversized hand were two blue pills. *He's so big. It's a bit like being nursed by a Wookie,* she thought to herself, stifling a giggle. It would be rude to laugh in the man's face when he was being so kind to her.

"These will help you sleep and help with the pain," he said. "Open." She obeyed without thinking, again responding to his dominant aura and authoritative tone. He placed the pills on her moist, pink tongue, his fingers grazing her lips as he did so, then held the sippy cup up for her to wash them down with.

"There," he said as she swallowed them. "How is your wrist feeling?"

"Numb," she said. "Better." He took the pack

of frozen peas off her wrist and examined it closely. As he studied her wrist, she was surprised at how gentle such a large man could be, his fingers just barely applying pressure as he held her arm. He ran his fingertips lightly over her skin and nodded.

"Doesn't seem to be broken but we can't know for sure until we can get it x rayed. Try to get some sleep. I'll be in to check on you again in a few hours." He got up to go, taking the package of peas with him.

"Wait, how did you know my name," she asked, suddenly realizing that she had never given it to him.

"Oh," he said, scratching his head again. It seemed to be a nervous tick of his. "I had to look at your I.D. for the hospital. They wanted your name and some other info. Sorry, I wasn't trying to be a creep, I promise."

"It's okay," she said sleepily. "You were just trying to help." As she closed her eyes again, he took a few more steps toward the door, treading as softly as he could.

"Micah," She called out weakly, already drifting back off to sleep. He hesitated in the doorway.

"Yes, lit - Lana?"

"Thank you for taking care of me."

"You're very welcome. Sweet dreams," he said quietly. He turned off the lights and closed the door quietly behind him.

Chapter 3

Lana woke up to the feeling of Micah's hand on her forehead. His fingers sought out the pulse on her neck and paused there, counting the beats. Her eyes fluttered open, and he smiled at her.

He has such a nice smile, she thought groggily. She felt caught in his gaze like a deer caught in the headlights, his green eyes twinkling in the low light.

"How are you feeling?" he asked, his voice full of concern.

"Hot," she said, suddenly noticing that she was drenched with sweat. She tried to kick off the blankets, but the minute that she moved, she froze. In her sleep, she had wet her diaper. The synthetic material was sticky and moist between her legs and, as she moved, the smell of urine wafted up. She cringed, hoping that he hadn't noticed.

"What's wrong?" asked Micah, sensing the sudden tension in the air. Lana felt her entire being burning with embarrassment. When she didn't answer right away, Micah's voice grew slightly panicked. "Are you hurt? Lana? Talk to me!"

"No, I'm not hurt, I just need to get to the bathroom." She knew that she was blushing, but she hoped he would just chalk that up to modesty. He was visibly relieved, his shoulders sagging as he let out a small sigh.

"Oh, of course! Sit up slowly, and I'll help you get down the hall. It isn't far." He put his hands under her shoulders and lifted her up. A wave of dizziness washed over her, and he held her up as she took a moment to get used to sitting upright. Eventually, the dizziness faded, and she was able to swing her legs off the edge of the bed and gingerly put her weight on her feet. As soon as she did, shooting pain in her ankle made her cry out and she sat back down on the bed hard, instinctively clutching at it.

"What happened?" asked Micah. His hands flew to the ankle she was grasping, wrapping his hands gently around hers. "Is your ankle broken? Let me see." He gently removed her hands, examining the swollen joint, shaking his head with dismay.

"You won't be walking on this anytime soon, I'm afraid. It's very swollen. If you want, I can carry you and help you onto the toilet." She blushed furiously, knowing that would include pulling down her pants and discovering her secret. It was unavoidable. It would seem. She had to get out of this wet diaper, and for that, she would require his help. Still, she had managed to keep this tendency of hers a secret for this long and part of her had hoped that no one would ever find out, even if it were a stranger who she would likely never see again.

"Hey, there's no need to be embarrassed," he said, his voice gentle and warm. His kindness only made her feel more ashamed. This nice, handsome man was about to learn what she had kept from so many boyfriends all these years.

"No, you don't understand," she said, avoiding his gaze. "I don't need to go to the bathroom because ... I already did." She buried her face in the pillow, wishing the earth would open up and swallow her whole. Micah didn't say anything for a long time, which made her nervous. Was he mad? Stifling laughter in an effort to be polite? Trying to find the quickest way out of there? She wanted to know but didn't have the courage to lift her head and look him in the eye.

"So, do you need me to help you get cleaned up?" he said, finally. There was no ridicule in his voice, nor was there anger. She still couldn't look at him, but she answered him, her words slightly muffled by the pillow.

"I'm sorry." She was on the verge of tears, and her voice cracked. Micah put his hand on her chin, gently pulling her face towards him.

"Look at me. I can't hear you when you have your face in the pillow like that." She turned her face towards him, her eyes cast downward.

She would never be able to look him in the eye again; she was certain of it.

"I said, I'm sorry." Her lower lip trembled, and the tears threatened to flood out but she just barely hold them back. Micah's thumb gently circled her chin, and he sighed.

"I told you to look at me," he said firmly. She obeyed, unable to resist his dominant tone. Despite her deep shame, she managed to look at him. "There is nothing to be sorry about. You are hurt, and you need help. I'm here and capable of giving you that help. If the tables were turned, wouldn't you help me?" She nodded, staring at him with big watery eyes. The effect that he had on her was stunning. She felt like she had been hit by a truck. A big, sexy, dominant truck.

"See? Now, I'm going to take your pants off, ok? I'll be as gentle as I can be, but I need you to let me know if I hurt your ankle or anything else." She blushed but tried to be brave. "Ok, I will." He nodded and moved to unbutton her jeans but hesitated, his fingers lingering over the clasp. He cleared his throat and shifted his weight slightly, and Lana was sure that he was more uncomfortable than he was letting on. She picked up the pillow and covered her face with it, hiding from her humiliation. A second later, Micah picked up the pillow and looked at her quizzically. Just when she thought that she couldn't get any more mortified, here he was looking at her like she was a crazy person.

"What are you doing?" he asked.

"I ... I'm still embarrassed." Her face burned, and she knew that she was blushing deeply.

"I know, little one," he said gently. She gasped quietly at the term of endearment but brushed it off, ignoring the heat it made her feel inside. Everyone probably seemed little to Micah. It probably didn't have the same significance to him as it did to her. "But it has to be done. I promise I won't laugh or make fun. Ok?" She nodded, feeling a little bit better. He smiled tentatively and unbuttoned her pants. He tugged at the waistband and froze when he saw that instead of underwear, she was wearing a diaper. She had no idea what to say as he stared down at her, his jaw slack with surprise.

"I'm sorry," she finally said, desperate to fill the awkward silence. He shook his head slightly, coming back to the present.

"No, don't be," he said, clearing his throat again. "It's a good thing you had this on, actually." He pulled her pants the rest of the way down, gently and slowly. She winced slightly as he brought the pants over her swollen ankle, but the pain was minuscule compared to her embarrassment.

"Do you have a medical condition?" he asked, and she could tell that he was fighting to keep his voice conversational. She appreciated the effort, amazed once again at his kindness towards her. "I'm sorry if that was a rude question, I just need to call the doc back if that's the case." She blushed and covered her face with her hands, groaning. It was tempting to use a fictional illness as an excuse, but she didn't want to lie to him.

"No, that's the worst part of all of this. I just like wearing them. I was feeling sorry for myself about the breakup, and so I wanted to wear one on my vacation to make myself feel better. I don't usually use them, I just." She trailed off and started crying. Hearing the words out loud was just too much, and she couldn't hold them back anymore. He perched next to her on the bed, taking up what little space was left and lifted her up, folding her in his arms. They felt so good around her, so strong and safe.

"There, there," he said soothingly. "It's ok, little one. Let it all out." He rocked her back and forth, holding her until she stopped crying and rubbing her back lightly to calm her. Eventually, her sniffles and sobs stopped. She pulled back slightly to see that she had soaked the front of Micah's shirt and was doubly mortified.

"Don't worry about it," he said gruffly, following her horrified gaze to the wet stain on his chest. He pulled a tissue from a box on the nightstand and gently wiped her face with it. He held it up to her nose and commanded her to blow. "Listen to me, Lana. No, don't look away. Look at me and listen. Don't ever be ashamed of being a little, ok? There is nothing wrong with you. There is no reason to be ashamed. Ok?" As the meaning behind his words began to sink in, it was her turn to stare at him in slack-jawed amazement.

"You know what a little is?!" He gently laughed at her astonishment. She would have felt embarrassed, but she somehow sensed that it wasn't mockery but rather a kind of admiration that had him so tickled.

"I do. I'm a Daddy Dom. Or weren't you wondering why I had a little pink sippy cup and no kids?"

"Well, no, actually. I - " She was at a loss. The odds of two people with the same sort of secret running into each other so far away from civilization were astounding.

"I happen to have some diapers and other things left behind by, a former companion of mine.

I could go get them if you like."

"Um, yeah, actually. That sounds really nice. If you don't mind sharing, that is." He smiled and lowered her back onto the bed, pulling the covers onto her legs. She couldn't help but notice how his hand lingered a bit on her thigh as he smoothed the covers down. Just that small amount of contact from him was enough to make her shiver all over.

"Not at all. Sit tight," he said with a wink and left the room. Her heart pounded as she waited for his return. She had never actually someone else that shared her preferences before. Not in real life, anyway. She had met a few friends online, but this was a whole new experience! This could actually be something. She had already been attracted to him before this revelation. His rugged, mountain man vibe was hard not to like after all. But she hadn't really given him that much thought since she probably wouldn't see him again after he took her to the hospital. Now, she suddenly felt nervous and excited. A real-life Daddy! The warm feeling she had gotten in her tummy was growing stronger. And lower. She blushed, embarrassed by her own body's reaction to a man she hardly knew. *Don't get ahead of yourself, Lana.*

He returned with a diaper bag and a stuffed bunny rabbit. She grinned when she saw the rabbit and forgot to be nervous for a moment. Stuffies were a huge source of comfort for her, and she had been secretly longing for hers, which had gotten left behind in her car. She had only brought two along for the trip, but they were her favorites, and she'd had them for years.

"I thought you might like to make a new friend," Micah said.

"Oh, I would! What's his name?"

"Well, as a matter of fact, he just told me the other day that he didn't like his old name anymore, can you believe that? Said he wasn't going to answer to it anymore. I think you should give him a new name. What do you think?" She giggled, her mood steadily improving as her crush on him got just a little bit bigger.

"Hmm. I think he looks like a Bernard," she

said after a moment's consideration. He held the bunny up to his ear, pretended to listen, then nodded.

"Bernard says he likes that." He gave her the stuffed bunny, and she held it close. A wave of comfort and relaxation came over her as she could feel herself enter her little space. The best part was, she didn't have to hide it around her new friend. She could openly be little and not have to worry. It was liberating.

He pulled a fresh diaper from the bag as well as some wipes and powder. Her eyes went wide, and she remembered to be nervous again. He pulled the covers back, and she couldn't help but notice the way his eyes lingered over her puffy diaper. She wondered what he was thinking but was too shy to ask.

"Have you ever been changed by anybody before?" he asked, his voice low and silky.

"No, I usually just do it myself."

"Well, lie back and relax, sweetie. Let me take care of you." His voice was so gentle. She found herself relaxing against the pillows and letting her knees fall open He loosened her diaper and began pulling it down. "Lift your hips. There's a good girl." His praise made her glow with pride. He pulled the diaper off, bundled it up, and put it in the trash. He kept his eyes averted to her exposed nakedness, pulling a wipe from the pack and draping it over her private area before using it to clean her up. It felt nice against her skin, cool and soft, and it was very hard not to think about how there was only a thin piece of cloth between them. Her face grew hot as she imagined him touching her down there for real. He tossed the wipe in the trash and pulled a new diaper from the pack, scooting it under her bottom. With a quick sprinkle of powder, he had her fastened back up in a flash. He pulled a bottle of hand sanitizer out of the bag and gave his hands a quick once over. He pulled the cover back over her and sat beside her, stroking her hair tenderly. His hands still had a lingering smell of alcohol, but she found that she didn't mind.

"See, that wasn't so bad, was it?" She smiled up at him, clutching Bernard tightly to her chest.

"No, that wasn't bad at all. It was really nice, actually." He returned her smile and brought his hand down to her cheek, stroking it lightly. She closed her eyes and nuzzled her face into his hand, beginning to feel the pull of the sleeping pills once again.

"How is your ankle feeling?"

"It still hurts," she said drowsily. "But I'm fine."

"We had better put some ice on it," she heard him say and felt him get up from the bed. In his brief absence, she drifted off to sleep again but woke up with a start when the frozen peas touched her inflamed ankle. "I'm sorry, little one. Go back to sleep."

"But it's cold," she whined and clutched Bernard tighter.

"I know it is, sweet girl. Just close your eyes, you'll forget all about it soon enough." He stroked her hair as he spoke, and her eyes fluttered closed.

As he petted her hair, he began humming a lullaby, and within minutes, her breath was coming slow and even. Micah tiptoed out of the room to let her rest.

Chapter 4

When Lana woke up again, it was morning. Well, almost morning. The first golden rays of dawn were just beginning to break through the grey night. She smelled the pungent odor of coffee wafting in from the next room and sat up excitedly.

"Micah?" she called out, wanting to let him know that she was awake. She sat up, searching for her pants which were on the floor near the door. As she put her foot tentatively on the floor, she heard him call to her from the kitchen.

"Hey! I thought the coffee might wake you up. How do you take yours?"

"Cream and sugar, please," she yelled back and tried her weight on her injured ankle. It hurt too much to walk on, so she decided to try hopping on one foot over to her pants. It went pretty well for about three and a half hops before she fell to the floor with a crash. She landed badly on her already injured wrist and yelped in pain. Micah came bursting into the room seconds later and rushed over to where she was lying on the floor, clutching her arm to her chest.

"What happened? What were you doing?" She pointed weakly to her pants, suddenly painfully aware that she had only a diaper and a t-shirt on and probably looked completely ridiculous sprawled out on the carpet. He looked at her with a combination of anger and concern on his handsome face. "Why didn't you call me?!" Before she could even answer, he had scooped her up from the floor and carried her as though she weighed nothing at all over to the bed. His brow was furrowed with concern as he studied her injured wrist for a moment before growling in frustration.

"I don't even know what I'm looking at!" He ran his hands through his shiny black hair in frustration. "The sheriff said the roads won't be cleared for another hour or so. You need a doctor now!"

"It's ok," she said, trying to calm him down. It was sweet that he was so concerned for her, but it was making her feel a tad guilty. She should have known better, should have just waited on him to help her get dressed. "I just jostled it a bit. Honestly, it's fine." He didn't look convinced, however, and looked at her with a cloud of anger on his face.

"Don't lie to me, little one," he growled, then softened as she pulled away in fear. "I'm sorry Lana, I should have taken better care of you. It's my fault you got hurt, not yours. I shouldn't have snapped at you like that."

"Don't be ridiculous, Micah," she put her good hand over his." You've done nothing but look after me since you found me yesterday. Hell, you were even making me coffee when I fell. It's my own stupid fault. I'm always doing dumb stuff like that." He shook his head, remorsefully.

"You know, if you were mine, you would have earned yourself two punishments already today, and it's not even breakfast yet."

"I - I would?!" She stared at him, wide-eyed.

"Yes, ma'am. One for getting out of bed when you're supposed to be resting and two for talking badly about yourself. No little girl of mine would be allowed to call herself dumb or stupid."

"You would really punish me for that?"

"You bet your little bottom I would! I'd make it a bad one, too. Stand in the corner with a bar of soap in your mouth, and that's just for starters." She swallowed hard and looked down, suddenly feeling abashed. The last thing she would ever want to do is disappoint him. That in and of itself was very telling, she realized.

"Please don't be mad at me," she said quietly.

"Oh darlin'," he said softly. "Daddies don't punish because they're mad. They punish because they want to look out for you and keep you safe."

"Really? I've never had a Daddy before." The confession slipped out before she even realized what she was saying. She hadn't really intended on telling him that but there it was.

"You haven't?!" It was his turn to be shocked. "But you're so perfect!" She blushed, and he looked away, scratching his head nervously. She wasn't used to being complimented so blatantly, but she liked how warm it made her feel inside.

"I've had boyfriends. I've just never told any of them about, you know …" She trailed off, still a little embarrassed about what she was even though she knew it was silly. After all, he was the same way.

"About being a little?" he finished for her. He nodded sympathetically. "It can be scary, I know. I've had more than one woman head for the hills after I told them that I'm a Daddy. But I still feel like honesty is the best policy. Better to be honest and upfront about what you want than end up unhappy and with the wrong person. Which is why you would actually have three punishments because you lied about your wrist being ok just a few minutes ago." She pulled Bernard closer to her instinctively as if he could protect her from these hypothetical punishments.

"You wouldn't even go easy on me for lying to make you feel better?" He shook his head firmly.

"Absolutely not. If you're hurt, you'd better tell your Daddy right away. Your comfort and safety are more important than anyone's ego. In fact, if he doesn't do everything in his power to make it right, then he ain't worth the name Daddy, you understand me, little girl?" She nodded at him, wide-eyed, and bit her lip. The forceful tone in his voice made her whole body go hot, and she suddenly felt lost in his sea-green eyes.

"Let me hear you say it," he said, giving her a hard look that said that he meant business.

"I understand, Micah," she said in a soft, shaky voice.

"Good," he said sighing. "There are a lot of predatory creeps out there who like to call themselves Daddies and I'd hate to see you get mixed up with one of them. But never mind all that, we'd better get you dressed so we can get you to the hospital."

"Will you -" she hesitated and blushed.

"What is it, baby girl? You can ask me." She could feel herself getting wet when he called her baby girl, and she stammered for a moment before she could regather her thoughts.

"Will you help me out of my diaper? I don't want the people at the hospital to see."

"Of course, I will! You'll have to go commando, though. I didn't think to grab your bag from the car. Sorry, I didn't know about the mudslide yet, I was just thinking about getting you to the hospital."

"That's ok. It's only for a few hours." She lay back so that he could loosen her diaper and scoot it off of her. Maybe it was her imagination, but she thought she saw him sneak a little peek this time around. So maybe she wasn't the only one feeling the chemistry. She had a wild urge to spread her legs for him and show off, something that was very out of character for her. Now was definitely not the time for that, anyway. Quickly, he slid her pants on and helped her get them over her hips.

Once they were on, he seemed a bit more relaxed. He helped her sit back up and went to get a comb for her hair. Delicately, he ran it through her gnarled knots until it was shiny and smooth. Lana was at a loss for words. She had never felt so pampered before. She loved the gentle way he ran his fingers through her hair and how close he was to her on the bed. She could feel his warmth radiating from him, and she wanted to lean into it and be wrapped up in his arms again.

"I'm sorry that I don't have a spare toothbrush or anything," he said, breaking the comfortable silence.

"That's ok," she said dreamily. She was so enraptured by his brushing that her mind felt a million miles away. He stopped combing her hair and touched her forehead, concerned.

"Are you ok? Is the dizziness coming back?" She snapped herself out of her reverie.

"Oh no, I'm fine, I was just spacing out a little." He squinted at her skeptically. "Are you sure? You aren't fibbing again?"

"No, I promise. No fibbing." She made a little X over her chest with her finger, crossing her heart. He laughed and nodded, throwing his hands up in mock surrender.

"Ok, ok, I believe you." He looked at her and seemed almost sad for a moment. "Well, the roads should be just about cleared up. We need to get you checked out by the doctor, and I don't want to wait for another minute. Sit tight while I get the truck warmed up."

He got up from the bed but lingered by the doorway. "Stay put, little one," he said firmly.

"I promise," she said sweetly, noticing the way his cheeks turned a little pink at the lilting tone in her voice.

Quit flirting. She chastised herself. *He doesn't want a dumb baby like you.* Then she realized that he might, actually. Except he wouldn't like it if she called herself dumb, he had said so himself. Lana flushed at the possibility of having a real-life Daddy of her very own before she put the thought out of her head.

Even if he were interested, which wasn't a guarantee, she was only here for the summer. And she'd just had her heartbroken. Nothing about this was practical or sensible. She could practically hear Barb now, telling her that a fun summer fling was just the thing to get over a broken heart, but that just wasn't Lana's style. She was the type who only had sex when she was in a committed relationship, one that had the potential to last beyond a few weeks.

On the other hand, maybe it's time for a change in style, she thought as Micah came back and bent down to take her into his strong, burly arms. Again, he scooped her up as if she weighed nothing. It was thrilling to be carried like that. He carried her with such ease that she felt like she was flying as he carried her to his truck.

He sat her down on the front seat and buckled her in. They drove in silence as Micah navigated the narrow mountain path. The road Lana had come in was a fairly wide dirt road but what Micah's hunting lodge was on could charitably be called a path. They turned a sharp corner and the trees cleared. Suddenly Lana could see how high up the mountain they were. It had been so dark when she came in last night that she didn't get to fully appreciate the landscape. She gasped as she saw a deep valley below them, blanketed in pine trees.

"How high up are we?" she asked, her nose pressed up against the window.

"Not that high, actually. The mountains in Georgia are at a low altitude compared to other mountain ranges because they're older."

"They're still higher up than anything you'll find in Florida." She clenched her eyes shut as they went around another steep curve in the road and suddenly questioned if the breathtaking view was really worth it. At least she didn't have to drive. She would be in tears, trying to navigate these narrow turns. They hit a hole in the road, and she squeaked loudly. He put his hand out and put it on her knee, and instantly her fear melted away.

"Are you ok, little one?" Every time he called her that, her body felt warm and glowy all over. She cleared her throat and nodded.

"Yes, I was just startled." His hand lingered on her knee, and she found herself hoping that he would leave it there. He hit a slippery patch on the road, however, and needed both hands on the wheel. She noted with a thrill that he gave her leg a little squeeze before removing his hand. They encountered a few downed limbs along the way, one of which was so big that Micah had to get out of the truck to move it, but for the most part, the roads were a lot more drivable than they had been the night before. Soon, they connected with the paved road which then connected to the main road into town.

As they pulled into the hospital parking lot, Lana swallowed hard, dreading what was coming next. This was probably the last she would see of Micah, which made her sadder than she was prepared for. She had no idea how to initiate a summer love affair, but she was pretty sure a hospital parking lot was not the best place for it.

"Well, thanks for rescuing me. I don't know

how I can ever repay you." Reluctantly, she put her hand on the handle to get out.

"You're welcome but don't think for one second that I'm going to let you hobble into the hospital by yourself. Stay put." He came around and lifted her out of the truck, carrying her all the way inside. Again, he had struck her speechless. She really didn't know what to say in response to such kindness. To her surprise, he stayed with her, even after they got her a wheelchair. He stayed while she waited for a room and while the doctor took a look at her. He stayed in the room when they wheeled her off for x-rays and was even still there waiting for her when they got back.

The doctor came into the room after a long wait to say that nothing was broken but that she would need to stay off her feet for a few days. With plenty of rest and ice, it would heal fairly quickly. As she wrote Lana some prescriptions, Micah announced that he would pull the truck around. When they wheeled her out, he lifted her out of the wheelchair and back in his truck.

"Where is the cabin you rented? We need to get you tucked back into bed right away." She blushed, a little flustered at how much attention he was showing her. Mike probably would have just dropped her off and then called her a cab if this had happened while they were still together. Lana gave him the address and tried to come up with the words to express her gratitude. She snuck little peeks at him while they drove, flushing every time she looked at his handsome face and found herself wondering what it would feel like to be pinned down under his massive frame. She had always had thoughts like that but had never had the courage to ask for it. Something told her that with him, she wouldn't have to ask and that just made the thought all the more thrilling. She got so lost in that thought that before she knew it, they were pulling into the rental office.

"Sit tight. I'll grab the key from the dropbox," he said. As he walked away from the truck, Lana couldn't stop watching his firm backside and muscled thighs. On his way back, she noted how nice the front view was as well. His jeans were hugging his package tightly. He handed her the keys as he got back in, brushing her fingers with his. Just that slight contact was enough to make her feel an ache between her legs.

"I'll drop you off, I'm sure you're beat, and then go back into town to get your prescriptions filled."

"Thank you, Micah. Really, I don't know what to say. You've been so kind to me." He reddened and seemed at a loss for words himself, scratching his head in that embarrassed way that he had.

"Oh, I couldn't just leave you stranded," he said, seeming to shrug it off. He didn't seem to realize that most people might have done exactly that. The fact that he didn't know what a special soul he was just made him even more endearing to her. He would never lord it over her or ask for special favors in return for being a decent human being. It was a refreshing change of pace for Lana. He found her cabin easily, just a couple of miles from the main office. It was a tiny little thing, advertised online as a lover's nest, a prefab affair made of pressed fiberwood made to look like a log cabin. He unlocked the door and turned on all the lights before coming back to carry her inside. He took her straight to the bedroom and gently lowered her onto the bed. For several minutes, he fussed around with pillows and blankets, making sure that she was comfortable. He brought in a glass of water and set it down on the bedside table.

"I'll be back in a couple of hours, do you need me to carry you to the bathroom before I go?" She shook her head. One of the many tests at the hospital had been a urinalysis, and she didn't have to go again just yet. He brushed her hair back and nodded. His hand on her forehead felt so nice that her eyes fluttered closed and she smiled before she could catch herself. She was exhausted and just wanted to curl up in his arms and sleep the rest of the day away.

"Ok," he said softly, his voice sounding suddenly thick with emotion or possibly just lust.

Maybe it was just her hopeful imagination. "I'll go by your car and get your bags out so you'll have everything that you need. I can call a tow truck when I get back and have it taken to a shop. With any luck, they'll have it repaired by the time you're back on your feet."

"You're so good to me," she said drowsily, already half asleep. He tucked her in and went to leave but hesitated for a moment. He bent down and kissed her forehead softly before leaving quietly. Lana fell asleep with a very big smile on her face.

Chapter 5

Micah tried to will his erection away as he drove into town, but thoughts of sweet little Lana plagued him all the way back to town. The fact that she was sick and injured did little to stop him from imagining her pretty pink lips wrapped around his cock which just made him feel all the more guilty for having those thoughts.

She doesn't need you creeping on her right now, he told himself. He couldn't help but kiss her on her forehead when he put her to bed. She looked so sweet and angelic lying there. The kiss had put a smile on her face, and that left him with the hope that there could be something between them someday, but right now she needed to rest and heal. He turned on the radio and hoped that would be enough to distract him. Unfortunately, every song seemed to be a love song, and that only reminded him of her.

He finished his errands as quickly as he could, eager to get back to check on Lana. She had already proven herself to be stubborn and hard-headed in the short time he had known her. He wasn't prepared for the way his heart had dropped when he came in and saw her crumpled on the floor, clutching her arm in pain, and he hoped like hell that he wouldn't return to find her like that again.

Despite his impatience to get back to Lana, he decided that he had better stop for groceries and supplies on the way back to the cabin. Once he was back, he didn't intend on leaving her again. Not for a very long time.

***

Lana woke up to the sound of Micah's tires crunching on the pebbled driveway. It seemed to her that he just left, but the dusk outside her window told her many hours had passed. Her bladder was feeling the effects of the passage of time as well. She squirmed under the covers, waiting for Micah to come inside and help her.

She heard him come in through the front door and set down several bags before going back out to the truck to bring in several more. She couldn't be patient anymore. She felt like she was bursting.

"Micah," she called out when she heard him come back inside. "I need you." He came hurrying in, turning on the light. The look on his face was one of worry, and that filled her heart with a warm glow.

"What's wrong, princess?" She gaped at him for a moment. The affectionate nickname seemed to short-circuit her brain.

"I - I - " The words seemed to have gotten stuck in her mouth, and she could only stammer inarticulately. He crossed the room quickly, a concerned look on his face, and frantically felt her forehead.

"I'm ok. I just need help going to the bathroom." Finally, she was able to speak. Micah looked relieved, as though he had been imagining the worst.

"I can do that. Let's get your pants off, little one." She clutched the covers to her chin.

"Can't you just carry me in and let me take care of the rest?" He shook his head.

"Nope, you could fall trying to scoot your pants down. I can't take that chance." She saw the logic in that and reluctantly lowered the sheets. "Don't worry. I promise not to look." He pulled the covers off her and gently began to take off her pants, helping her scoot them over her hips and delicately folding them and putting them on the bed next to her.

"So you don't have to go hopping all around looking for them later," he said. True to his word, he lifted her out of bed without taking a peek. The air was cool on her butt as he carried her, and it felt strangely nice to be exposed that way. Maybe it was because it was usually covered, but the skin on her butt seemed to be extra sensitive. He slowly and gently lowered her onto the seat and stood there, waiting. The urgent need to go was suddenly replaced by a consummate shyness as Micah watched her expectantly.

"I can't go if you watch," she said blushing. "Can I have a moment of privacy, please?"

"I'll turn around, but I don't want you to be by yourself if I can help it. I would never forgive myself if you fell and got yourself hurt again."

"I'm not gonna fall," she muttered. He turned around, his face to the wall, but that's as far as he went. She rolled his eyes at his back and decided that if he wanted to stay, then she wasn't going to let that stop her.
It was easier to go once he was no longer looking. She finished up as quickly as she could and flushed the toilet.

"Can I turn around now?" he asked, almost sounding hurt as if she had banished him to the corner like a scolded child. She wondered what he would look like with a pouty lip and tried not to giggle, knowing that would only add insult to injury.

"Yes, you can turn around now," she said, barely managing to keep a straight face. He didn't have pouty lips when he turned around but it was pretty close. Gently, he lifted her back up and carried her back to bed. She reached for her pants but he stopped her with a gentle touch of his hand.

"Wouldn't you rather wear a diaper, little one?" She looked away, still embarrassed that he knew her secret. He gently nudged her chin, pulling her face back toward him. "What's wrong, you're not still feeling embarrassed are you?" For some reason, she suddenly felt on the verge of tears and couldn't answer. She knew it didn't make sense to be ashamed in front of someone who had the same tastes as hers but after a lifetime of hiding it, she was finding it hard to be comfortable with someone knowing. He sat on the bed next to her, looking her deep in the eye.

"Would it help you to know that I find you very sexy in your diaper?" His voice was quiet and husky. She swallowed hard as a wave of heat washed over her entire body. She could only nod as she looked at him wide-eyed. He smiled at her, then picked up her hand and kissed the back of it, keeping her gaze locked onto his green eyes the entire time.

She felt her body flush with heat again, most of all between her legs. No man had ever turned her on so much just by kissing the back of her hand. No man had ever made her feel as intoxicated as he did. Her heart pounded. She hoped that he would kiss her on the lips next, but instead, he got up and came back with a bag of diapers. Again, he averted his eyes as he diapered her. She appreciated him being a gentleman, but at the same time, she wanted to grab his hand and put it between her legs and beg him to ease the ache that had been growing there all day. Or better yet, to hold her down and fuck her into the mattress.

She was so lost in that last thought that he had the diaper in place and was covering her back up with the blanket before she even realized it.

"But I'm not sleepy," she said, looking up at him with big eyes, hoping he would take the hint.

"Doesn't mean you're not staying in bed. Are you hungry? I got you some soup and some mac and cheese. I wasn't sure what all else you like."

"I like chocolate," she said hopefully. It was no toe-curling sex, but it would do for now. He laughed and shook his head.

"Yeah, I figured as much, but that's for dessert. You need something real for dinner." The stern look on his face told her that there was no point in arguing.

"Mac and cheese?" He nodded, deeming that an acceptable choice.

"Coming right up, Princess." He went out to the kitchen and got things going. When he came back, he had a book and a box in his hands. "I saw this adult coloring book and some pencils at the grocery store, so I picked them up. Don't want you going stir crazy up here." He winked as he put them both down on her lap and her stomach did somersaults. She opened the box of pencils. Her face lit up when she saw all the pretty colors. She flipped through the book excitedly, trying to decide which one to color first. Micah watched her for a moment with a smile on his face, enjoying the sight of her enjoying herself, then went back to making dinner. When he returned with a bowl of hot, cheesy noodles, she had already finished half of a mandala.

"Ok, little one, put the coloring away. It's dinner time." She looked disappointed for a moment, but then she smelled the mac and cheese, and her tummy rumbled, reminding her that she had not eaten that day. She reached for the bowl, but Micah put it on the table. "The bowl is hot, be careful."

He picked up the fork and scooped out a bite, carefully blowing on it before bringing it delicately to her mouth. She instinctively opened her mouth and let him feed her. He was already scooping up a second bit before she actually processed what was happening.

"You don't have to feed me, you know," she said, trying to sound more grownup than she felt at that moment.

"I know that, but I'm going to anyway," he said firmly, bringing the fork to her mouth once again. "You need someone to take care of you and not just because you're injured. You just got your heart broke, and you're up here all alone. I want to show you that not all men high tail it and run as soon as things get tough."

She ate in silence for a while, her mind a whirlwind of thoughts. After a few minutes, she finally worked up the courage to ask the question that had been on her mind all day.

"Do you mean ... you want to be my Daddy?" He lowered the fork and just looked at her for a moment, his beautiful green eyes had her caught like a deer in the headlights. The question hung in the air and for a moment, Lana's stomach dropped, certain that she had misread something and had offended him greatly. Instead of answering, however, he leaned in and kissed her very softly. His lips were warm and so inviting, she opened up to him without hesitation. He broke off the kiss way too soon for her liking, and she whimpered softly as he pulled away. He ran his thumb over her bottom lip and smiled.

"Yes, baby girl. I would love to be your Daddy." Lana could only stare at him, feeling slightly dazed as though she were in a dream. She knew she should say something, but he had once again rendered her speechless. He was good at doing that, she noted.

"Cool," was the most eloquent thing she could summon to say in response. Inwardly she cringed, feeling like the most awkward person on the planet. He only smiled, seemingly pleased with the response, and continued feeding her. After she finished her dinner, he made her drink an entire glass of water before she could have the chocolate he had gotten her for dessert.

"Aren't you going to get some dinner?" she asked as she happily munched on her treat.

"I will after I've taken care of my princess," he replied. She almost choked on her chocolate. That was easily the most romantic thing anyone had ever said to her. He took the chocolate away after she had only eaten a couple of pieces.

"That's enough for tonight," he said, kissing her on the forehead before she even had a chance to complain. He gave her back her coloring book and pencils. "Finish up your pretty picture while Daddy eats his dinner and cleans up. I'll be back soon."

She colored happily as he went back to the kitchen, her mind full of dreamy sweet thoughts about her new Daddy.

Chapter 6

He came back sometime later. Lana was so wrapped up in her coloring that she wasn't sure exactly how long but she had finished the first mandala and was almost done with a second one.

"It's bedtime, baby girl," he said. "Time to put the coloring away."

"But I'm not tired, Daddy," she said. Her eyes did feel a little on the heavy side, but she was too excited about the recent turn of events to sleep. How could she relax when her stomach was so full of butterflies every time he looked at her?

"Here," he said, handing her a handful of pills. "These will help the pain and help you sleep." She swallowed them all down with a few sips of water. He took the cup from her and put it back on the nightstand. "I can take you to the bathroom before you go to sleep if you want. Or you can use your diaper again tonight if you need to. Don't be shy. Daddy loves changing your diaper for you." Her heart fluttered again. She never thought that she would hear those words, much less than from someone so handsome and kind. How did she get so lucky?

"I'm ok for now. I'll use my diaper if I need to." While Lana didn't usually wet her diaper, she usually just liked wearing it, she did like being changed by Micah. It also had the added benefit of being practical while she was recovering.

Besides, maybe he won't look away now that he is my Daddy. The thought made Lana burn with desire. She imagined herself splayed out before him as he lovingly caressed every inch of her. Her body was flooded by a sudden urgent need.

"Daddy ..." She wasn't sure exactly what to say, how to voice the fiery desire that now gripped her.

"What is it pumpkin?" he asked, sitting on the bed next to her and taking her hand. She wanted him to pin that hand down to the bed, push her legs apart and take her but she knew they shouldn't do that, not yet anyway. It was too soon for her, summer fling or not and she didn't think it would be as much fun while she was injured anyway. But she needed more than that one little kiss from earlier.

"Can I ... can we kiss some more?" She blushed furiously as the words came out. He made her feel so bold and shy at the same time. He grinned at her, and she could feel her heart glowing.

I had better watch myself, she thought. *This one is dangerous.* It would be oh so easy to let herself fall in love with this charming, dominant, Southern gentleman. Especially if he kept flashing her that grin and giving her butterflies just from holding her hand. Even knowing that it was a bad idea that would likely end in heartbreak might not be enough of a deterrent. She would gladly take the heartbreak if it meant giving in to him.

"Just for a minute, little one," he said. "Then you have to get some sleep." He gently caressed her cheek, studying her face. Then, he brought his hand down to under her chin and lifted her face to him. His lips took hers hungrily as he held her face, his tongue bursting into her mouth, tasting her greedily. He kissed her with such fire and passion that it took her breath away and she could only cling to his shirt as he claimed her with his mouth. The heated wetness between her legs only grew worse as she opened herself up to him, surrendering herself to his demanding tongue. When he broke off the kiss, Lana audibly groaned with disappointment. She needed more, a lot more. Micah only laughed and shook his head, however.

"No, little one. It's time for sleep, and if we keep doing that, neither of us will get any sleep at all tonight. Daddy will read you a story if you'd like, that should help you relax. I picked up a romance story and a mystery story, which one would you like?" Lana considered it a moment before deciding that the romance story might make it even harder to sleep than it already would be after that panty-melting kiss. Hearing about the strong hero seducing the vulnerable maiden would only make the heat between her legs grow worse, especially if it was coming from Micah's lips.

"Mystery story, please." Micah nodded and opened the book, clearing his throat before beginning. She lay back and closed her eyes, listening to Micah's soothing velvety voice. She listened until her body quieted, and she was able to sleep.

***

Micah put the book down and quietly tiptoed out of the room. Lana was finally breathing long and even. As he sat down on the couch that would serve as his bed that evening, he felt his cock throb uncomfortably in his pants. It had not gone down since that deep sexy kiss from his baby girl, even after reading to her for almost half an hour. Watching her sweet face as she drifted off to sleep had done nothing to remedy the situation either. He shifted himself on the couch, trying to find a comfortable position so that he could relax and get some sleep.

He had not planned on things progressing so quickly. He had wanted to wait until she was better healed. She would need to be in good health to endure the things he was planning on doing to her. All he had been able to think about was all the different ways that she could pleasure him and all the different ways that he could make her cum. It was going to be all the harder to resist her if she was going to be asking him for kisses like that. He cursed under his breath and took his throbbing cock out, spitting into his hand. He was going to have to relieve this tension if he was going to keep his hands to himself.

All he could think about was having Lana's sweet lips wrapped around his cock, moaning softly as she licked and nuzzled his shaft. He had accidentally caught a peek of her little pink pussy earlier, and it had driven him wild ever since. Now he imagined her completely naked, on her knees before him. He ached to fondle her perfect perky breasts as she pleasured him slowly and sensually, licking every inch of him with her sexy pink tongue.

A ragged sigh escaped his lips as he stroked himself slowly, enjoying the mental image. The fact that she had never had a Daddy before was strangely intriguing to him, and he looked forward to showing her all of the fun that could be had. He wanted to show her how to live the lifestyle safely and healthily but, more selfishly, he also wanted to train her on how to be a good little for her Daddy. He tried not to think of it as training her for himself. She would be back in Florida by the end of the summer. That thought was just a little too much reality at the moment. Better think about how much fun they could have for now, how cute she would look begging him for his cum and how even cuter she would look with it sprayed all over her pretty face. The thought was too much for his lust addled brain, and he was cumming just as soon as he pictured it.

My princess, he thought as he erupted,

coating his hand, shirt, and pants with his hot, sticky jizz. He sat there, breathless and gripping his still-hard cock, dreams of Lana still running through his head. It had barely been enough to take the edge off, but it would have to do for now. He cleaned himself off quickly and collapsed onto the couch, hoping to rest.

Chapter 7

Lana slept most of the time over the next few days, and Micah was beginning to go a little stir-crazy with no one to talk to. He risked going back to his cabin to get a few books and other things to keep him entertained but only after making Lana pinky promise not to move from the bed before he got back. She promised him and swore to be a good girl, and he believed her, already trusting her implicitly even though they had known each other for a very short time.

On the way back, however, he regretted that. She was so sleepy from the pain medicine that he was scared that she would roll out of bed by accident. He kicked himself for being selfish and leaving her there all alone, certain that he would return to find her crumpled on the floor once more. Of course, all the worrying was for nothing. She was still tucked safely away in bed when he got back to the cabin. As he sighed in relief and rushed to her side, he silently swore to himself that he wouldn't leave the cabin again until she was completely healed.

Within a few days, Lana was feeling better enough to complain about being bored. He let her sit on the couch and watch TV but still insisted on carrying her around wherever she needed to go and waiting on her hand and foot.

"My ankle doesn't even hurt that much anymore," she had complained when he still wouldn't even let her go to the bathroom by herself.

"Not good enough," he had said. "Talk to me when it doesn't hurt at all anymore. Until then, you're not walking anywhere." She knew she should have hesitated at that, telling him that she was a grown woman who could damn well take care of herself, but the truth was that she melted inside over how special it made her feel to be babied to this degree. It was easy to tell that his overprotective behavior came from a place of genuine concern. He was constantly checking on her comfort levels and asking her if there was anything she needed. She had never felt like the center of anyone's world before, and it was a feeling that she hoped she would have to get used to.

Bath time was awkward. He had offered to bathe her, but she felt like that was perhaps too intimate too fast, at least for her. And she'd only hurt her wrist and ankle, after all. It wasn't strictly speaking necessary. As pleasant as it sounded to be bathed by him, she wanted the first time he saw her completely naked to be under somewhat more romantic circumstances. The compromise was that Micah would place Lana in the empty tub fully dressed and she would undress and fill the tub. It was admittedly a little weird, but it would work, for now, they decided.

They snuggled on the couch, spending their days in quiet companionship. Micah read and Lana colored most of the time, or they would watch a movie together. They kissed every so often, but Micah always stopped her when she tried to take it further.

"Don't you want to?" she had asked, frustrated by how slow he wanted to take things. She was usually the one who wanted to slow things down, not the other way around. It was a bit bruising to the ego. He had taken her face in his hands and looked deeply into her eyes before responding.

"Baby girl, of course, I do. The problem is, once I start, I'm not going to stop. Daddy is going to fuck you over and over until I'm satisfied. I'm going to make you come so hard and so often that you're not going to be able to remember your own name. So get your rest now, little one. You're going to need it." He had run his thumb lightly over her bottom lip and then kissed her softly. Lana felt like her whole body was on fire, just from a few simple words. No one had ever spoken to her that way before. Sex had always been a quick activity before bed. Micah made it sound like an all-day event. She wanted so badly for him to push her down onto the couch and take her then and there but he only calmly went back to his book as though he were in no hurry whatsoever.

Finally, the day came for her follow up appointment with the doctor. Micah drove her into town, stopping for some ice cream on the way to sooth Lana's nerves. She didn't have a full-on phobia of hospitals or anything, but she had confessed to him a few days before that doctors made her a little bit nervous. The fact that he remembered and wanted to help her feel better absolutely melted her heart. The doctor gave her a clean bill of health and told her that she could walk on her ankle again and do light activities. She would still take it easy for a while, however, nothing too strenuous.

"Can she have sex?" Micah interjected. He had been sitting quietly in the corner of the room up until that point. The doctor looked a little confused but replied that she didn't see any reason why not. Micah only nodded and didn't have anything else to say for the rest of the appointment. He let her walk on her own pack to the truck but insisted that she take a hold of his arm, just in case. Lana's foot felt one hundred percent better, but she was happy to be able to hold on to his arm for other reasons.

They drove back in silence. Lana wasn't sure what Micah was thinking about but she certainly only had one thing on her mind. The wait was finally over. The doctor had said so herself, and she could finally get what she had been craving for the past several days. Micah, and a lot of him.

She snuck a peek at him, but he seemed as calm as ever. Feeling bold, she reached over and put her hand on his leg. He kept both eyes on the road but took one hand off the wheel to hold hers, squeezing it firmly. He didn't let go for the rest of the drive.

Chapter 8

They had barely taken two steps into the cabin when Micah grabbed her by the arm and pulled her close to him. He wrapped her in his huge arms and looked down at her, drinking in every detail of her face before kissing her deeply. His hungry tongue pushed into her mouth and tasted her like he was starving for her, his arms gripping her so tightly that she could barely breathe. She opened up to him, moaning into his mouth as he explored her with his tongue. His hands began to explore her body as well, running over the curves of her hips and butt. He started to reach under her top but stopped, pulling back from the kiss.

"Get in that bedroom right now, little girl," he growled. Lana's knees instantly grew weak in response to his sexy dominance, but she did as she was told, scurrying off to the bedroom as quickly as she could with Micah right behind her.

"On the bed," she heard him command from behind her as he closed the bedroom door. She kneeled on the bed and waited for him. It was almost dusk now and she just barely could see him, waiting by the door in the shadow.

"Take off your shirt," he said, his voice so low and demanding it sent shivers through her. This was so completely new to her, being told what to do in bed, that she hesitated for a moment. "Baby girl, I expect you to do what I say when I say it. Is that understood?" She nodded, the words filling her with a needy heat and making it hard to think. He seemed to radiate lust and dominance, and it made her feel almost intoxicated by him. This was what she had been longing for her entire life, and it was finally happening.

"Let me hear you repeat it. I want to make sure you truly understand what I'm telling you." His voice was almost a whisper now, but every fiber of her being was attuned to him, waiting for what he would tell her to do next, eager to obey him. It was like a compulsion within her.

"I will do what you say when you say it." Her voice sounded dreamy and distant; the demanding need between her legs only growing stronger. As she said the words, she felt the weight and the significance of what she was promising, and it excited her. She couldn't wait to be his, really and truly his.

"Good," he purred. "Now take off your shirt like a good girl." She pulled the t-shirt over her head and tossed it to the floor. He didn't say anything for a moment, just drank in her naked body in with his eyes.

"You're so beautiful, baby girl," he said, making her blush deeply. No one had ever looked at her so intensely before, and it was making her feel self-conscious. Hearing his reassuring words made her glow with pride even through her bashfulness. She had never tried to be provocative before so she moved on instinct, running her hands slowly over her stomach and hips for his visual pleasure. Judging from the sharp inhale from Micah, it worked.

"Take off your pants," he growled. The whisper was gone, his voice now thick and velvety, and she imagined him as the big bad wolf, lurking in the shadows. Slowly, she unbuttoned her jeans, unpeeling them down her hips. Even though she couldn't see his eyes, she could feel him track her every move. Knowing that he was watching her, aroused by her was such an aphrodisiac. She lay back on the bed and kicked her pants off and lounged back on the pillows, savoring the feeling of anticipation that sent tingles all over her.

"Open your legs," came the next command. "I want to see what is mine." Slowly, she parted her knees, thoroughly intoxicated by his domination over her. Her pussy was dripping wet already even though he had barely touched her. She was fairly certain that she would be able to see how aroused she was from the dark spot left by her juices. He made a noise somewhere between a moan and a growl and rubbed his cock through his jeans but made no move to take them off or come towards her.

"You're mine now, baby girl." His voice was hypnotic, thick with lust. "Every part of you, every inch of you now belongs to me. Do you understand me?"

"Yes, Daddy." Lana felt breathless. Her body yearned for him more powerfully than she ever thought was possible.

"I want to hear you repeat it, little girl. What are you?"

"I'm yours. I belong to you, every inch of me."

"That's right, little one. Now let Daddy see those perfect tits." Lana gasped as her core clenched with desire and she hurriedly obeyed, eager to give him whatever he asked for. As she tossed the bra aside and proudly displayed herself for him, she heard him growl "good girl," and she was filled with glowing pride. His praise erased all self-doubt. At last, he came towards her, his slow sensual movements heavy with the promise of things to come. He had a raw hunger on his face that made her tremble inside, made her need to be consumed by him. He joined her on the bed, kneeling in between her legs, and gazed down at her. With a contented sigh, he ran his hands over her breasts. Her nipples hardened and came alive under his touch, and his grasp became firmer, more demanding. He bent down, claiming her mouth briefly with his own before working his way downward, devouring her neck and breasts. He teased her with his lips and tongue, nibbling lightly at her flesh. His hands continued to explore her body as well, pulling her hips against him so that she could feel the bulge of his cock against the thin material of her panties. Lana threw her head back against the pillows, moaning with delight as he lavished her body with attention. As he slid his hands over the outside of her panties, she was overwhelmed by the pleasure that washed over. The way he gripped her lightly, feeling her wetness against the palm of his hand, felt so deliciously possessive. She ground her pelvis against his hand, her body seeking more to satisfy its urgent craving. He chuckled with his mouth around her nipple.

"Are you already that needy, baby?" he asked, his voice teasing and playful. "Daddy has just barely gotten started with you, little one." As he spoke, he hooked his fingers into her panties and peeled them down until they were past her feet, tossing them aside. He grinned like a satisfied cat as he looked at her, now completely naked. She felt exposed and vulnerable in a way that made her body flush with desire. If she wasn't able to relieve some of this pressure soon, she felt like she might lose her mind. It had been building between them for so long that it was now an all-consuming need. He lowered himself on the bed, putting his face so close to her pussy that she could feel his breath against her. He stared at her adoringly and traced a finger lightly around her labia, the gentle touch making her thighs quiver. Slowly, he explored her with his finger, tracing over her folds and dipping into the wetness pooled in between, staring at her intently the entire time as if he were memorizing her. She squirmed and moaned as he teased her, the soft sensations not nearly enough to quell her craving.

"Tell Daddy what you need, little one," he purred, grinning up at her, clearly enjoying the sight of her writhing and moaning. Her body cried out for relief, but the thought of putting it into words made her burn with embarrassment. His finger hovered near her entrance, waiting.

"Please, Daddy," she gasped and yearned her hips forward, desperate to be filled by him, to ease the ache within at last.

"Not until you tell Daddy what you need. You can ask me for anything, baby girl. Just say it." Lana found that she was beyond caring. She had no time for modesty anymore. Her body was on fire, and only one thing could sate her.

"Please make me cum, Daddy. I need you so badly, please!"

"Good girl," he purred as he slipped his finger inside of her at last, never taking his eyes off her as she threw her head back and moaned in sweet relief. Still looking up at her, he put his warm, soft tongue against her aching clit, moaning against her as she gyrated her hips. He pumped his finger in and out of her, hitting her most sensitive spot with every thrust into her hungry pussy. She watched him as she slid her clit up and down his tongue, working herself towards an orgasm. She had never seen a man so happy just to give her pleasure before, and she couldn't take her eyes away. She clutched the sheets of the bed. Her thighs clenched as she worked herself against his tongue, frantically meeting the thrust of his finger deep inside of her. All at once, she came on his tongue, ecstasy moving like an unstoppable force from the center of her being and rippling all over her. She clutched the back of his head, pulling him closer as she climaxed, and he pumped his finger into her harder. When she finally relaxed back against the mattress, breathless and panting, he gave a deep, satisfied sigh.

"You taste so good, baby girl." He nuzzled her clit again, making her jump slightly. "I could stay down here for hours and hours." Gently, he kissed the spot just above her clit, making her twitch slightly, then got up to his knees. He stripped his shirt off, revealing a broad, hairy chest, thick arm muscles, and toned abs. Everything about him was so attractive to her, just looking at him drove her wild. He looked so delicious that she had to sit up and run her hands over his chest and abs, appreciating his masculine form.

"Daddy, you're so sexy," she whispered and slowly began to kiss his stomach, her hands reach for the clasp on his jeans, ready to claim her prize.

"Thank you, little one," he said and sighed in pleasure as she unzipped his pants, her tender lips inching toward the elastic band of his underwear. His hands ran gently over her hair as she began tugging on his jeans and underwear, unable to get them over his hard, muscular thighs. "Need some help?" He lay back on the bed, effortlessly kicking off his pants and spread out on the bed, displaying his nude form for her to enjoy.

He looked completely comfortable being nude, even seemed to enjoy having her eyes on him. She thought that on any other man, that kind of confidence would have come across as arrogant but on Micah, it was incredibly alluring. His cock was enormous and already throbbing, and she longed to have it inside of her, to show him the same pleasure that he had shown her. Gazing at it with a slightly dazed hunger, she stroked it lightly with her hand, enjoying how his face went slack with pleasure at her touch.

"Daddy's turn," she purred and bent down to kiss the tip lightly. She closed her eyes as she tongued the underside of the tip, savoring the taste of him. He put his hand under chin, lifting her face slightly.

"Look at me," he said. She opened her eyes again to see him staring down at her with an intensity she had never seen before. Her face got hot with embarrassment, and she suddenly felt very self-conscious. "Keep going, little one. Daddy wants to watch you suck his cock, don't be shy."

She smiled, his naughty words filling her with encouragement, and took the tip of him into her mouth. His breath quickened, and he stroked her cheek, gazing down at her with open adoration. Keeping her eyes locked on his, she began to work his shaft further and further down her throat, getting a thrill from the look of agonized pleasure on his face. That look emboldened her, made her begin to pick up her pace with enthusiasm, loving the effect she was clearly having on him.

"Stop, baby girl," he suddenly growled, pulling her up. She almost whined with disappointment, but he pulled her up for a deep kiss, his erection pressing between them as he held her close. She melted against him as his greedy tongue pushed into her mouth, his teeth lightly grazing her lip. "You almost made me cum, little one. I'm not done with you yet." He grabbed a handful of her hair and tugged her head to the side, exposing her neck. He held her like that as he kissed and bit her neck, making her squirm with desire. Despite the powerful orgasm she'd had just minutes before, her body was already on fire, yearning for more. She gripped his broad shoulders as he devoured her neck, moaning softly as the mild pain in her scalp only intensified her need. She felt helpless pinned against him like that, and that helplessness was exhilarating.

With his free hand, he grabbed the flesh of her buttocks, digging his fingers into the skin as he pulled her closer against his throbbing member. With a vicious growl, he brought his hand down sharply onto her ass, spanking her forcefully. Lana was not prepared for the pain or the way it made her body clench with the desire. She moaned loudly as he brought his hand down, again and again, keeping her pinned against him with his fist in her hair. The flesh of her buttocks stung more and more with every blow, and she could feel her pussy responding with an aching need. She spread her legs, straddling him, and started squirming against him as he spanked her. Her body sought out what it needed, inching him closer and closer to her entrance, desperate to have him inside of her. He growled in her ear, bringing his hand even harder down onto her buttocks.

"What is it that you're after down there, little one? Hmm?" She knew he wanted her to voice her need once again, but it was impossible to think when he was spanking her so firmly, much less speak. She whined and writhed against him, but he only spanked her again, his blows beginning to come harder and harder. Part of her wanted to stay like that forever, locked in perpetual anticipation as he masterfully teased her, inflaming her desire.

"Tell Daddy what you want," he said, his tone indicating that he was losing patience. She opened her legs wider as the tip of his cock brushed her labia. He was so close to being inside her. It would take just a tiny little thrust. But he had her locked in place with his strong arms. She could not wiggle her way onto his cock. He would not give her what she so desperately needed until she asked for it, but his methodical spanking filled her head with a fog of pain and pleasure, too adrift in a sea of bliss to move. *The sweetest torture*, she thought distantly, feeling as though she had entirely lost control of her body. Suddenly, he shifted her weight, flipping her onto her back and kneeling between her knees. She gasped loudly as he began to run the tip of his cock over her clit, rubbing it in slow circles over her swollen nub.

"Do you want Daddy's cock, little one?" he said with a husky voice. She stared down, fascinated by the sight of his cock gliding over her, and nodded. "Say it." She no longer felt frozen, the sensation of his rigid member against her aching sex demolished all of her inhibitions and the words came tumbling out at last.

"I want your cock, Daddy. Please, I need it, please fuck me!" With a satisfied sneer, he plunged into her, roaring with satisfaction as he buried himself inside of her to the hilt. Lana made a roar of her own, grasping his buttocks to pull him closer. Her entire body felt alive as he stretched her open, taking her hard and fast. He unleashed his passion onto her, rutting into her like a crazed animal. His hands twisted into her hair, yanking her hair back as he drove himself into her furiously.

"Is that what you wanted, kitten?" he growled into her ear.

"Yes, fuck me hard!" Lana had never experienced such heat, such passion, and she wanted it to go on and on. As his thick cock split her open again and again, she could feel another climax building. She raked her nails over his back and buttocks, wild with pleasure.

"Good girl," he laughed playfully. "Let it all out, princess." He reached down and began to stroke her clit with his thumb as he pounded into her, overwhelming her with ecstasy. The double stimulation was too much for her, and another orgasm broke over her, stronger than the first, as she thrashed her head from side to side. She let herself go completely, trembling and moaning beneath him.

"Oh fuck, baby girl, you're so tight around my cock." As Lana's quaking orgasm began to recede, Micah's thrusts quickened. She could feel his manhood grow even harder inside of her, throbbing on the edge of release. "Look at me." Shyly, she peeked up at him. He yanked her hair harder to bring her face closer to his, holding her face firmly with his other hand. The possessive way his fingers dug into her face gave her a sense of belonging that she never thought possible before that moment.

"You're mine," he said, holding her gaze with his sea-green eyes. "Say it." She felt her heart melt open in a way it never had before, leaving her feeling raw and vulnerable. Every cell in her body knew it was true, knew that this man was her future.

"I'm yours, Micah," she whispered. He pulled her face to his for a kiss, deep but tender.

"All mine," he whispered, his breath hot against her lips. His rhythm suddenly faltered, and she could feel his grip on her hair tightened as his body went rigid. His cock throbbed and twitched inside of her as he filled her up with his seed. With one final shudder, he collapsed against her and buried his face in her neck, his breath ragged. They clung to each other, Lana surprised at how comfortable she was with Micah's weight on top of her. His arms gripped her tightly, holding her close against her body as he lay with his still-hard cock inside of her, seemingly in no hurry to move. She had never felt so safe, so contented. She held him close and kissed his sweaty forehead, brushing his hair aside as he caught his breath, and thought about how she would love to stay like that forever.

Chapter 9

When Lana woke again, it was pitch black dark outside. Micah was sprawled out on the bed beside her, naked and snoring softly. She felt a wave of affection suddenly, coupled with a desire that had only been partially quenched by their lovemaking earlier. As quietly as she could, she lowered herself until her face was level to his member. Even soft, it was impressive to look at, laying across his toned belly like a python lying in wait. Gingerly, she took the head into her mouth, barely applying pressure as she ran her tongue over the sensitive tip. He made a soft noise but didn't open his eyes. As she took him further into her mouth, she could feel his cock begin to twitch as the blood flooded in. He still tasted of their shared juices, and she moaned lightly as she tasted him. As he grew harder, she began to apply more pressure, delighting in how responsive he was. With a happy sigh, he finally opened his eyes. Looking down at her with sleepy affection, he smiled and ran his fingers lightly through her hair.

"Are you already greedy for more, little one?" he purred. "Mmm, I love seeing you so needy for my cock." Grabbing a handful of her hair, he pushed her down further onto him, his partially erect member sliding easily down her throat. It was delightful, feeling a fullness in her throat without feeling like she had to gag, and she swallowed him greedily. As he grew fully erect, she struggled to keep him down her throat, choking slightly around his thick member. He stroked her face as she pleasured him, testing her own limits as she took him deeper and deeper.

"Oh fuck, kitten!" Micah threw his head back against the pillow. "That's so good. You're doing so good. Yeah, choke on it, baby." Lana felt almost hypnotized, her body tingled with desire as she gagged and choked on him. Never before had she gotten such satisfaction from giving a blowjob, had never felt this desire to consume someone entirely like she did with Micah. His obvious enjoyment egged her on, made her want more and more of him.

"Princess, you're going to make me cum," he groaned, gripping her hair harder. "Do you want Daddy to cum in your mouth?" Lana nodded and began sucking him off faster, stroking his balls lightly with her finger tips. She stared at his handsome face, enjoying the look of ecstasy on his chiseled face as he grunted and filled her mouth with his cum. She swallowed it all eagerly, moaning quietly as he held a fistful of her hair, holding her down on his pulsing cock.

"Good girl," he whispered shakily, patting the back of her head gently. With a happy grin, she gently licked up a few droplets of cum that hand landed on his stomach before curling up into his arms. He kissed her, his breath still shaky, and reached down to stroke her aching pussy.

"Oh, sweetie, you're so wet," he purred with a grin. "Why don't you get on up here and sit on

Daddy's face?" Before she could respond, he was grabbing her by her ass and hoisting her up so that she was straddling his shoulders. With a squeal and a giggle, she scooted up so that his tongue met her clit. He gave her pussy a long slow lick, moaning with satisfaction as he tasted her. She grabbed a handful of his silky black hair and ground her hips against him. He grabbed her by the wrists and moved her hands to her bare breasts instead.

"Play with your titties, Pumpkin," he whispered. "Show Daddy how you like to be touched." He went back to twirling his tongue around her clit as she groped herself, pinching her nipples as he studied her closely.

"Harder," he commanded. "I want to see how hard you can take it." She twisted her nipple, the pain combining with the delicious sensations of his tongue lapping at her, and she moaned, grinding herself against his mouth. He grabbed her by the ass, his fingers digging into her flesh as he devoured her.

"Slap your tits," he growled and flicked his tongue lightly across her clit. Tentatively, she smacked her palms on her nipples, intrigued by the sensation. "Harder," he pushed, and she obeyed. She slapped her breasts, again and again, each time a little more forcefully as she found that the pain mixed with pleasure was bringing her close to a climax. He groaned approvingly and smack her ass hard, adding to the intense sensations. She felt her legs grow shaky as she squirmed against his mouth. As he brought his hand down onto her fleshy buttock once more, she could hold back no longer. She twisted her nipples, harder than ever before as wave after wave of intense pleasure washed over her. He grabbed her hips, holding her firmly down on his mouth as she shivered and quaked, her moans echoing off the walls of the small bedroom. As she collapsed back, he caught her, gently easing her down on the mattress. She sighed happily as he wrapped his arms around her again, kissing her deeply. She could taste her own juices on his tongue, and she moaned into his mouth, feeling dirty in the best possible way. She loved the way he stripped her of her inhibitions, making her submit entirely to his desires, opening her up to a whole new world of pleasure.

To her surprise, Micah was already hard again. Eating her out must have aroused him greatly because she could feel him begin to press into her, ready to claim her once again. She opened her legs wider, eager to have him inside of her. She was still sensitive from her climax and shivered with delight as he thrust into her.

"Oh, baby girl, you're so wet," he exclaimed, "Keep taking it just like that. Oh, you're such a good girl." His thick cock claimed her, affirming that she belonged to him. She moaned and grabbed his ass, pulling him deeper inside of her, craving more of him. He seemed to know all the right spots to hit and, even better, made sure to hit them with every stroke.

"Daddy, you feel so good," she cried out, thrashing her head against the pillow as he split her open again and again. With a sigh, he pulled out, grabbing her by the hips and flipping her so that she was up on all fours. Something about the way he manhandled her, putting her exactly where he wanted her, made her feel like his sexy little plaything. As he entered her from behind, she noticed that it was a different sensation. He seemed to fill her up more, going deeper with every thrust. He grabbed her hand, guiding it to touch her clit as he pounded into her.

"Does that feel good, sweetheart?" he asked, grabbing the flesh of her buttocks and pulling them apart.

"Yes, Daddy," she said, rubbing her sensitive spot as his rock hard cock stretched her out.

"Oh princess, your tight little pussy is milking my cock. You're so tight and wet, just for me." She felt him run his thumb over her other entrance and shuddered, totally unprepared for the toe-curling jolt it sent throughout her body. "Do you like that, baby girl?"

"Ooh, Daddy!" she cried out, rocking her hips back to meet his. "Oh, that feels really nice." She had never been stimulated there before and had never thought that she would like it, but as Micah ran circles around her rear entrance, it made her pussy react. He licked his thumb and slowly began to sink it in, moving gradually to allow her body time to adjust to the intrusion. The anal stimulation was sending her close to another orgasm, and she squealed and squirmed with delight, rubbing her clit furiously.

"Oh, kitten, you're so tight. Are you going to come on Daddy's cock again?" She couldn't answer, she could only moan and rub her clit as she clenched around his cock and thumb, orgasming with such force that her legs shook. As her climax subsided, he hammered into her even harder, his thumb digging further into her ass. She started to pull her hand away from her clit, but he slapped her ass hard, making her yelp with pain, and grabbed her wrist, replacing her hand between her legs.

"Did I tell you to stop touching yourself, baby girl?" he growled, smacking her ass again. Lana's eyes rolled back in her head, the thoughts in her head too jumbled from the overwhelming pain and pleasure.

"N-no, Daddy," she managed to stammer out. Obediently, she began running her finger over her sensitive nub once again, trembling with pleasure and he claimed her body with his.

"I told you, once I start fucking you, I'm not going to stop. I'm not going to stop until you can't think or stand. You'll only be able to lay there and take it." She shivered, the image was enticing. Already she felt beyond all words and thought. As she grunted and thrust back against him, she felt like a wild woman, all inhibitions thrown to the wind. It felt so right and natural to give over control to him, to be his puppet made only to please him. The thought made her pussy clench, and she knew that she would soon be orgasming again. He spat on her rear entrance, giving his thumb more slip as he began to work it in and out of her. It was by far the dirtiest thing anyone had ever done to her in the bedroom, and she was shocked to find that she didn't find it disgusting. Rather, his ownership of her allowed her the freedom to be as dirty for him as he wanted her to be.

"Oh, Daddy," she squealed. As both his thumb and his cock slid in and out of her, Lana came so hard that her voice broke and her legs collapsed beneath her. Micah was undeterred, shifting his weight so that he was on top of her and just kept right on fucking her into the mattress just as she had dreamed that he would. She kicked her legs and squealed, the stimulation was too much to handle, and she felt like she was losing her mind.

"So naughty." He groaned and swatted her ass again. "Keep rubbing that clit, little one. If I have to tell you again, I'm going to strap a vibrator to your leg and keep it there all night." Lana obeyed at once, dreading what that much stimulation would do to her already taxed body and mind. She rubbed her clit, helpless against the onslaught of pleasure as Micah continued to use her without mercy. She whined and moaned, her skin growing slick with sweat as she thrashed and kicked underneath him. Just as she was beginning to think that she couldn't take another climax, Micah pulled his thumb out of her ass and replaced it with the tip of his cock. He pulled her hips up and swatted away her hand, touching her clit directly with his large fingers. Slowly, he began to push himself into her, stretching out her rear end with his thick cock. He was slick with her juices and slid in easily yet was careful not to go too quickly lest he hurt her. Lana screamed and thrashed underneath him. It felt more amazing than anything she ever experienced before, so amazing that her tired, over-stimulated body was somehow building to yet another orgasm. He pushed himself past the rim, her tight ass hugging the tip of his cock as he rubbed her clit, driving her mad with pleasure. She thrust her hips back as she got closer, wanting to take more of him inside of her. He let her control the pace, letting her fuck herself with his cock as he rubbed her closer and closer to cumming. She thrust herself all the way back, taking him completely inside her body, and shook with an orgasm so powerful that she couldn't move or make noise, she could only lay there and quake beneath him. It seemed to last forever, her body rigid with ecstasy, but at last, she came down from the peak, utterly exhausted.

"Oh baby girl," he cried out, pulling himself from her With a loud grunt, he let himself go, spraying her back with his cum. It felt so warm as it hit her flesh, so possessive, as though he were marking her as his. The thought sent a contented wave of happiness over her, glowing with pride at being owned by him.

He collapsed his weight onto the bed beside her, lazily wrapping his arm around her waist and pulling her close. She felt like her entire body was made of jello. She felt sore and exhausted but also happier than she had ever felt in her life, and he put his hand on the back of her head and stroked her hair.

"Oh, baby girl. You did so good. Daddy is so proud of you." He held her face up to his for a kiss, his warm lips gentle and soft against hers. She melted into him, savoring the warm feeling of skin on skin. Moving seemed completely out of the question, so they lay in each other's arms for a long time as he stroked her back and hair. Eventually, he disentangled himself from her with a groan, stretching languidly before padding into the kitchen, still naked. He returned with a large glass of water and instructed her to drink all of it.

"You're going to need to stay very hydrated. Daddy has big plans for you over the next few days." The way he said it made her tummy do flips wondering what else he could possibly have in mind. After she finished her water, he tucked her back into bed. It wasn't yet daylight, and they were sure to be able to catch a few more hours of sleep. After he got back into the bed with her, she curled around his large frame once again.

"Get your rest, little one. You're going to need it." He chuckled and kissed her forehead. She smiled and closed her eyes, looking forward to whatever came next.

Chapter 10

True to his word, Micah was hungry for more first thing in the morning. He woke her up by licking her pussy, telling her that they wouldn't be getting up for breakfast until she had five orgasms. At first, she giggled, but by the third orgasm, she was no longer laughing, and by the fifth one she was on the verge of tears. He made her pancakes for breakfast, and they both ate in ravenous silence. As she watched Micah eat, she could feel her body responding to him. It was as though he were training her to associate him with pleasure. Lana smiled and turned her attention back to her plate. If that was the case, she thought, it was working. He suggested that after breakfast, they should go for a hike. The cabin she had rented was attached to a short private trail for the rental company's customers to enjoy.

"Not a long one, of course. We don't want to strain your ankle, after all. But it would be a real shame for you to spend your entire vacation cooped up inside. If you like it and want to try something more challenging or scenic, I know of some other trails around here that I can take you to as well." Lana had never been hiking before, but she was well up for the adventure. She only had a pair of tennis shoes which Micah said would be fine for today. If she eventually wanted to work her way up to a more challenging path, he said that he would buy her new hiking boots.

"You will?" She couldn't help her surprise. It wasn't her birthday, an anniversary, or Christmas.

"Of course, little one. I want to make sure that you have the proper footwear. I always want you to be safe and comfortable. Understood?" She nodded.

"I understand, Daddy," she said and stood on her tiptoes to kiss him.

"What was that for?" It was his turn to be surprised. She only shrugged and smiled at him.

"Just because you're cute." His face reddened a bit, and he scratched his head.

"Let's go, kitten," he said, putting his hand on the small of her back to lead her out of the cabin and into the fresh air. The small gesture was dominant in a nonsexual way that made her go a bit weak in the knees. It was a lovely day, lots of sunshine without being too hot. They stuck to the shade where the late spring air was still fresh and cool. The trail was fairly level and easy to traverse. He checked in with her often, offering to stop to let her rest or even carry her if she needed him too but she declined.

"Really, Micah, I feel fine. Stop worrying."

"Nope, not going to happen," he said and took her hand. "I'm going to keep right on worrying about you, and there is nothing you can do about it little girl." She giggled, glowing from within as he pulled her close to him.

"You are mine now," he whispered in her ear, his hot breath making her pussy clench with need as if he hadn't just spent the entire morning making her scream. He grabbed a handful of her ass, bringing the bulge of his cock against her stomach. She could feel herself getting wet all over again. He looked around surreptitiously to see if anyone was close by. When he saw that there was no one, he looked down at her with an evil grin before pulling her up so that she had to wrap her legs around his waist and carried her off into the trees.

"You are mine," he repeated, pushing her up against the bare trunk of a tree and sliding his hand under her shirt, grabbing a handful of her breasts. He tasted her mouth slowly and sensually, tweaking her nipples as he swallowed her moans. "Are you ready to show Daddy that you truly belong to me?"

"What do you mean?" she asked breathlessly. How else could she show him but what they have already been doing? What more of herself could she give?

"I'm going to use you for my pleasure. I'm going to fuck you and cum in that tight little pussy of yours, but you are not allowed to cum. I want you to still be wet and needy when I'm done with you, waiting desperately for me to use you again. Is that understood?" She gasped, her entire body aching at his words. It was so erotic, the thought of him having such absolute control over her body and mind like that, giving or denying pleasure at his whim. She shivered as the thought about being left wanting more, her craving for him only growing as the day went on.

"Yes, Daddy. I promise not to cum when you use me. I won't cum again until you tell me to."

"Good girl," he growled, putting her back down on her feet. "Now pull your pants down and turn around." Her clit was throbbing as she did what he commanded, her shaking hands pulling at the waistband of her leggings and panties, exposing herself to the daylight. She shuffled her feet, turning her face toward the tree and waited, her skin tingling with anticipation as she awaited his next instructions. He didn't say anything for a long while. She heard the sound of metal on metal as he unzipped his pants, but then there was only silence again. Curiosity made her want to turn to see what he was doing, but her need to obey him kept her facing the tree. He seemed to enjoy making her wait, knowing that the anticipation only made her want him more.

"Bend over," he said at last. She put her hand on the tree to steady herself and bent at the hips, giving him a full view of her pussy and ass. He made a satisfied noise, putting one hand on the silky skin of her bottom, giving her goosebumps as he just barely ran his fingers over her sensitive flesh. He pressed his hard cock against her clit, making her legs tremble slightly. He laughed as he tapped it against, making her jump and twitch with every tap.

"Oh kitten, you're already so wet and needy for Daddy's cock. You just can't get enough of it, can you?" She shook her head and groaned, squirming back against him. He brought his hand down onto her ass hard.

"Can you, kitten?" Instinctively, she knew

what he wanted to hear, and she found herself eager to say it, eager to do anything to please him.

"Please, Daddy. I need you to fuck me again. I need your cock."

"Good girl," he sighed, inching himself into her slowly. Her eyes rolled back in her head as he filled her in an agonizingly slow pace until he was buried in her completely. He held her there for a moment, grabbing her by the hips as he savored the feeling of being so deep inside of her. He began pulling out at that same excruciatingly slow speed. Lana acutely aware of every sensation as he slowly stretched her open, pleasuring her but also leaving her aching for more. Her body cried out for more, and she whimpered, moving her hips to increase the tempo. He only slapped her ass, however, and gripped her hips harder to hold her in place.

"What did I tell you, little girl? You had your fun this morning. Now it's Daddy's turn. Don't move until I'm done with you." Her pussy tightened around him, his words only making her crave him all the more. She whined and gripped the tree as he took his sweet time, seemingly not the least bit concerned that they could be discovered at any moment. She wondered what they would look like to a stranger who happened upon them, what they might think of her. Would they think she was a slut? For some reason, the thought sent a thrill through her.

"I'm sorry. I'll be a good slut for you, Daddy." It seemed to have a similar effect on Micah. He made a strangled noise and slammed his cock into her, suddenly pounding fast and hard, no more teasing. She held on tight, biting her lip to keep from crying out in satisfaction. Every thrust sent a lightning bolt of pleasure through her, and she focused her mind on his cock and the delicious fucking he was giving her.

"Good girl," he whispered. "That's a good little slut." Suddenly, he was pulsing inside of her, grunting as he pumped her full of his seed. With a shaky breath, he began to pull up her panties but didn't pull out just yet. He pumped his partially hard cock into her a few more times, clearly just enjoying the feeling of using her; however, he wished. It felt even more amazing, being fucked with a pussy full of cum, and her body wanted more and more. She felt like she would never get enough of him, no matter how many times they fucked. Finally, he pulled out of her, careful to catch all the semen that dripped out onto her panties. He pulled them up, caked with his cum, and then pulled her pants up as well. He pulled her against him, wrapping one arm around her waist as he kissed her from behind. With the other arm, he gave her pussy a light pat, and she could feel his little present squishing in her underwear. Her face suddenly felt hot, and she knew that she was blushing furiously. This was the kind of thing that Lana had always thought was gross and stupid when Barb would tell her about them. She loved Barb but had always thought that the things she let men do to her were crass and tasteless.

Looks like I owe her an apology, she thought as she squeezed her thighs together, savoring the sensation. He slipped his tongue into her mouth quickly before pulling his pants back up and winking at her.

"That was perfect, baby girl. You're so sexy." He wrapped his arms around her, holding her close. She was still aching for him, but she closed her eyes contentedly, enjoying the hunger. It made her feel so alive and so sexy. He took her by the hand, leading her back to the trail. With every step she took, she had a reminder of who she belonged to. She was sure that there must be a wet spot on her pants and blushed, part of her hoping no one would see while another, dirtier part of her hoped that everyone would. She wanted everyone to know who she belonged to.

Chapter 11

Back at the cabin, Micah said he would make up some lunch and that she should play until it was ready. After all of that physical activity, Lana found that she was starving. She stopped him on the way to the kitchen, however, wanting something else besides food.

"Daddy, will you put me in a diaper please?" She could feel herself going into her little space and wanted to experience that with him. He smiled and kissed her forehead.

"Of course, princess. Daddy will help you out of your sticky panties and into a nice, fresh diaper." She blushed at the reminder that her panties were still full of his cum and even more at how erotic she had found the experience. He was bringing out a whole new side to her, and it was thrilling. He picked her up and carried her to the bedroom, placing her gently on the bed. She lay back and let him take her pants off. He took a moment to admire the stain on her panties from his little present before removing them as well.

"Oh, baby girl, you look so sexy right now," he said as she opened her legs for him. "I can still my cum leaking out of you. You are so perfect." He took a wet wipe and began to delicately clean her off, moving it slowly over her labia as his breath began to quicken.

"Do you ever masturbate in your diaper, sweetheart?" he asked as he pulled one out of the pack.

"No, is that normal?" she asked. He smiled and shook his head.

"There is no normal. Everybody is a little bit different from the next person. I like the way you look in your diaper. I find it very sexy. But not everyone likes them for that reason. Some people just feel comfortable wearing them." She thought about it for a moment as he slid the diaper onto her and fastened it with elastic tabs.

"I think I'm a comfort person. I usually wear them when I'm feeling sad or stressed out, not when I'm feeling horny." He nodded slowly and put her pants back on her.

"Are you feeling sad or stressed out right now?" She considered the question thoughtfully then shook her head.

"No, I just want to be comfortable and be a baby for a while. It's fun and relaxing."

"Well, alrighty then." He kissed her on the forehead again. "Good to know."

"You're not upset that I don't want to do stuff in my diaper?"

"Upset? No, of course not. I still get the pleasure of seeing you happy. What about that could ever make me upset?" She didn't know what to say. He had that effect on her often, she realized, and smiled, kissing him on the cheek.

"Thank you, Daddy. Can I have my pacifier?" He chuckled and fished it out from the nightstand, placing it her mouth, then kissing the handle. Lana giggled, feeling like the luckiest girl in the world.

"Come on, cutie. You can color while I make us lunch." He carried her into the living room and put her down on the floor then brought her her coloring supplies and a couple of stuffies. He watched her play affectionately for a few minutes before going off to prepare their meal.

***

After lunch, Lana took a long nap and awoke to the sounds of Micah cooking dinner. She groggily stumbled into the kitchen to find him frying chicken.

"Hey kitten, you slept the whole day away. Feeling ok?" She nodded and grinned sheepishly. "Yeah. I guess you wore me out today." He laughed and patted the back of her diaper affectionately. "I warned you, little one. I've got an appetite."

"No complaints here." She helped him make dinner and set the table. After they ate, Micah took her hand and kissed it.

"Listen, kitten. My vacation is going to be over soon, and I'm afraid that I'll need to go back to the city."

"The city? Do you mean Atlanta? You don't live out here?"

"No, that's just a hunting cabin, remember?" She scrunched up her face as she recalled something to that effect. "I work as a lawyer in the city. I just come here to get away, but I have to go back to work. Would you want to come with me? There are a lot of fun things we can do in the city together."

"Yeah!" she said excitedly. "And I could stay at your place?"

"Of course, baby girl. Daddy's place is your place, anytime you like. I don't go back to work for a couple of more days, but we could head back to the city early if you'd like and I could show you around." A night of dinner and dancing sounded amazing to Lana. It had been so long since she had been out. Then she remembered that she had mostly only brought hiking clothes, thinking she would be spending most of her time enjoying the outdoors.

"I didn't bring anything dressy, though." She wrinkled her face at the thought of going to a nightclub in yoga pants.

"I guess I'd better take you shopping, then." Her eyes sparkled, and her face lit up.

"Really?!" He laughed and kissed her nose.

"Pumpkin, I would do anything if it meant seeing that look on your face. We'll make shopping our first priority when we get to town tomorrow." She truly felt like a princess all of a sudden. No one had ever offered to take her shopping before.

"Hold that thought," she said and scurried off to the bedroom. She dug through her suitcase and found her sexiest underwear. She stripped off her unused diaper and t-shirt, sliding on a red lace thong and a silky black bra. With a quick check in the mirror to make sure her hair wasn't too crazy, she went back into the kitchen to find Micah cleaning off the table. When he saw her, he put down the plate he was holding and let out a low whistle, looking her up and down with admiration.

"Damn, baby girl. You're making me hungry all over again." She smiled and did a little twirl for him, letting him see the back view as well.

"Do you like it, Daddy?" she asked. He crossed the small kitchen and picked her up by her bum, carrying her towards the couch.

"How about I show you how much I like it," he growled. He sat down with her in his lap, pulling her legs apart so that she was straddling him. He pulled her down so that he could kiss her neck, letting his hands wander freely over her body. She sighed happily and closed her eyes as he lavished her with attention. He unhooked her bra, staring at her breasts with a hunger in his eyes. Her nipples hardened with arousal as he stared at her.

"Push them together for me, pumpkin." She held her breasts and pushed them up and in, presenting them to him. "Good girl. You look so perfect like that." He buried his face in her cleavage, kissing, licking, and sucking the skin of her breasts with passionate abandon. He gripped her buttocks as he devoured her, grinding her already wet pussy against him. Her happy sighs turned to moans as he smacked her ass, lightly at first, but then with increasing intensity.

"Do you like it when Daddy spanks you, little one?" he murmured against her nipple. She moaned and squirmed against him.

"Yes, Daddy. Spank my ass, please." He grinned up at her, and her stomach fluttered with excitement. She had already learned that that grin meant he had a dirty idea. So far, she had liked all of his dirty ideas.

"I'm so glad that you said that Princess." He pushed her face down onto the couch, swinging her legs so that she lay across his lap. With one hand he held down both of her wrists, and with the other, he rubbed her backside lovingly. She whined and squirmed, feeling herself go from wet to dripping almost instantly. He suddenly slapped her ass three times in a row, harder than he had before. She gasped and jerked at the sharp pain, gritting her teeth as she fought to take it like a good girl. He chuckled at her response and caressed her flesh tenderly with his fingertips.

"What do you think of that? Do you still like it when Daddy spanks you?" Her hips thrust back, her buttocks seeking more of the pleasure-pain and she nodded her head, silently asking for more.

"Use your words, kitten," he said sternly, popping her already tender buttcheeks playfully.

"Yes, Daddy," she gasped, overwhelmed by her burning desire. "I love you. Please, spank me more!" She hid her face in the pillows of the couch as he delivered blow after blow to her meaty buttocks. She squealed and squirmed as he increased the intensity, each blow landing harder than the last, but she made no move to stop him. The onslaught ceased, and he once again stroked her tender flesh. She peeked at him over her shoulder, his face was flushed, and he was breathing heavily, his eyes fixated on her bottom.

"Oh, sweetie, your little bum is so pink," he said quietly. His fingers on her backside felt so good, and once again, her hips rose, giving him access to all of her. He pushed aside her panties and began to lightly trace her cleft, tracing all the way down to the very center of her desire. He gently exploring her folds, holding her gaze with his own as he touched her.

"You're so wet, you dirty little thing. You must like getting spanked a lot. Daddy is going to have to come up with some other way to punish you." He twirled his fingertips around her sensitive nub, making her eyes roll back in her head. She was so overwhelmed with the sensation that she could neither squeal nor moan, only grip the pillows and writhe in his lap. Just as she thought that it couldn't get more intense, he once again brought his open hand down on her tender rear end. She cried out as she lost all sense of control, surrendering completely to his mastery over her body.

"You're not about to come, are you princess?" He smacked her twice in a row, painful smacks that made her jump and gasp. "Because I haven't given you permission to cum yet." He plunged a finger into her aching entrance, bringing her closer to a screaming climax. It took all of her willpower to hold back as he pumped his finger in and out of her, rubbing her g spot with every stroke.

"Please, Daddy, it feels so good. I want to cum so bad." He didn't seem convinced and spanked her hard, sending sparks of pain all through her. Her tender bottom was beginning to feel raw and bruised, and her body was screaming for release.

"I think you can do better than that, little one."

"Please, Daddy. I want to come on your hand so bad. I've been a good girl. Please let me cum. Your finger feels so good inside my slutty little pussy. Please, Daddy, can I?" He didn't answer her, only slid a second finger into her, stretching her out. She kicked her legs and squealed, feeling incredibly full and closer than ever to coming without permission.

"Daddy, please, I can't take it. Please let me come!"

"Yes princess, you can come for Daddy." He smacked her ass as he pumped his fingers into her, sending Lana over the edge. Her entire body shook as fingers drove into her relentlessly, drawing every ounce of pleasure that he could from her climax.

"That's it, kitten. Let it all out, all over Daddy's fingers. There's a good girl." He did not let up until she had stopped quivering and twitching in his lap, utterly spent. He rubbed her butt softly as she lay there, too worn out to move. She gave a shaky sigh as he removed his fingers and brought them to his mouth, licking them with a satisfied moan.

"Oh, baby girl, you are so sexy. You taste so sweet."

"Thank you, Daddy," she slurred, her words muffled by the couch cushions.

"So adorable," he chuckled and pulled her back up to sitting, cradling her in his lap. She wrapped her arms around his neck and rested her head on his shoulder, enjoying the feeling of being completely safe in his arms. After a few minutes, she came down from her euphoria to notice his erection poking into her bottom. She squirmed against it, eager to show him the same pleasure that he had just shown her. He gasped and moaned, the movement seemingly catching him off guard. She grinned as she reached her hand down between them, feeling his hard cock through his jeans.

"Oh kitten," he sighed, catching her lips with his and gently biting her lower lip. As their tongues intertwined, she undid his belt and pants. She got down on her knees on the floor in front of him as he brought out his cock, bouncing with excitement. As she wrapped her lips around him, she made a happy little moan.

"Did you like deepthroating me the other day, princess?" he asked as she slid him in and out of her mouth.

"Yes, Daddy." Her lips brushed the tip of his

cock as she spoke, sending a shiver through him.

"Do you want to practice that some more? See how far we can fit Daddy's cock down that pretty little throat?" She smiled up at him, turned on at the thought. He was so responsive. It was an absolute joy to bring him pleasure.

"Yes, Daddy, that sounds really fun." He put his hand on the back of her head, silently encouraging her to take him deep into her mouth. She worked his shaft deeper down her throat until she began to feel herself gag. Undeterred, she tried to fit even more of him down her throat, choking so hard that tears sprang to her eyes.

"Whoa, slow down, kitten. There's no rush. Just take it nice and slow." He caressed her cheek as she caught her breath. "Are you okay? Do you want to keep going?"

"Yes, Daddy," she said, taking him in her mouth again. He whispered encouragement to her as he thrust in and out of her throat, holding her face gently.

"That's better. Just relax, baby girl. Let

Daddy slide in and out. Good girl, just like that." She let herself relax into it, his hypnotic pace and soothing voice putting her into an almost zen-like state. The more she relaxed, the deeper he pumped into her throat, and the better it felt. She could feel some drool begin to dribble out of her mouth and down his shaft, but she was so drunk on lust that she didn't care.

"Yeah, take Daddy's cock just like that, princess. You're doing so good. I love it when you drool on my cock, baby." She let a little more dribble out just to see the delighted expression on his face. "Daddy's dirty girl. You're going to make me cum, sweetheart." She caressed his balls, wordless encouragement for him to come in her mouth again. He had other plans, however, and grabbed her by her hair, pulling her off his shaft and standing so that he was looming over her. He worked his cock furiously over her open mouth and let loose all over her face and breasts. It was sensual and erotic, the way his hot seed rained down over her, and she caught as much as she could in her mouth, savoring the taste of him. He sat back down with a sigh, still gripping her tightly by the hair. He brought her face to his, kissing her deeply as his ragged breath came back down to normal.

"Oh, sweetheart, you're so sexy. You look so pretty covered in my cum."

"Thank you, Daddy," she said, glowing at the compliment. Indeed, she did feel pretty and sexy around him. He had a way of making sex not only satisfying but really fun and intimate as well. She felt so lucky as he bundled her up in his arms and carried her off to the bathroom.

He drew a bubble bath for her, stripping off her little red thong and holding her hand as she got it. The warm water felt amazing, and Micah's large hands began to massage her scalp, sending her even further into relaxed bliss. He scrubbed her skin clean with a loofah, taking extra care to be gentle on her tender and bruised bottom. Lana found that she rather liked the marks left by him. She loved having a tangible reminder of pleasure they had shared together and how it marked her as his. He washed her hair, rinsing out the suds with some water from a plastic cup. She leaned back, letting the warm water cascade over her hair. Once she was all clean, he spent a while rubbing her shoulders, letting her relax in the warm water while he eased any remaining tension away. Eventually, he let out the water and bundled her body and hair into towels before carrying her to bed.

"I'm not sleepy, Daddy," she said as he lowered her onto the mattress.

"Neither am I, kitten. Our night together is just getting started." He kissed her hungrily as he began to unwrap the towel from around her naked body.

Chapter 12

They slept in late the next morning, both of them were exhausted from a long night of lovemaking. Micah made pancakes while Lana packed an overnight bag. One quick stop by his hunting cabin to make sure it was locked and secure and they were on the road to Atlanta. He played some country music tunes on their way, and Lana took turns enjoying the scenery and snoozing in the passenger seat. It wasn't a very far trip, and before she knew it, they were in the city. They stopped by his apartment first to drop off their bags and freshen up after the trip. He lived in a high rise apartment in the downtown area of the city. The inside was nice, with industrial decor. Lana wouldn't be surprised if he had hired a professional decorator.

Once they were settled and unpacked, he took her

to a small boutique nearby and bought her a few dresses and a couple of shoes. She offered to pay for them herself, but he refused.

"I know how little office staff make. You hold onto your money, let me take care of it." He winked at her as he handed over his card to the cashier. "I was thinking that we could have some lunch and then afterward there is another shop I want to take you to."

"More dresses? Honestly, I think I have enough for now."

"No little one, not more dresses." He hadn't elaborated any further, leaving Lana to wonder. They ate at a small restaurant nearby, Lana having soup and salad and Micah having a Reuben sandwich. She wondered where he was going to take her next but didn't pester him about it, wanting it to be a surprise. Her time with him had taught her to appreciate how much sweeter a little bit of mystery and anticipation can make things.

It turned out to be a lingerie shop but one unlike

any that she had ever seen before. Upon their arrival, they were greeted by a personal shopper who offered them champagne. She took Lana's measurements and brought out a few samples for Lana to try on. Micah told her to take her time and to pick out whatever she liked.

"I'm sure whatever you choose will be lovely. I have some things I want to look at myself." Lana didn't have much experience with lingerie and relied on the shopper's opinion to make her decisions. She finally settled on three items that she thought Micah would enjoy and met him back out front. He had already rung up his items, wrapped and tucked away in bags so that she couldn't see them. More surprises.

Back at his place, he said that he wanted to take her someplace nice for dinner and that she should put on one of her pretty new dresses with something sexy underneath. After her shower, she picked out a black sheer bodysuit to wear underneath a purple form-fitting dress that hit just above the knee. She did her hair and makeup especially nice, happy to have a reason to wear a smokey eye for once. As she came out from the bathroom, Micah looked very happy to see her. His face lit up like a kid on Christmas morning.

"Oooh baby girl, you look good enough to eat. Come here." Lana giggled and came close to him. He held a box in his hand which he handed to her. "I have something to add to your beautiful ensemble." She opened the box to find a vibrator that was shaped like a large U so that it stimulated both the g-spot and clitoris.

"You want me to wear this during dinner?" she asked, confused.

"I do. I have the controls installed on my phone. You are mine, and I want to be able to play with you whenever and wherever I wish. Is that understood?" She flushed, her breath quickening with the thought. A dirty little secret that only the two of them knew about.

"Yes, Daddy," she whispered, nearly breathless with excitement.

"Let's see you putting it in, kitten." She smiled and reached under her skirt, unclasping the bodysuit at the crotch. Maintaining eye contact with him, she licked her fingers and slid them over her pussy and the vibe, giving it a little extra slip before sliding the vibe in. Once it was snugly in place, she snapped her bodysuit back into place. It felt strange between her legs yet not uncomfortable.

"Good girl. Now, let's try this out." He took out his phone and tapped the screen a few times. She felt a powerful vibration between her legs, making her legs quiver. A little squeak escaped her lips as she tried to maintain her composure. It hit both of her most sensitive areas at once, making it impossible to think, speak, or walk. He watched her intently, letting the vibrator go on for several seconds before stopping it with a few more taps on his phone.

"Goodness, how high did you have that up?" she said, trying to regain her breath.

"That was the lowest setting, little one." He

put his arm around her waist, pulling her close to him. She shivered as he brushed a strand of hair out of her face and looked her in the eye. "Now, since I'm a very generous man, I'm going to go ahead and give you permission to cum as many times as you need to, pumpkin." She flushed at the thought of climaxing in public and wondered how she would even pull that off. She was certain that she would look as though she were having some sort of fit. Given the strength of the lowest setting, she didn't think she would be able to stop herself from cumming, however, especially now that she knew that was his goal.

"Thank you, Daddy," she said, smiling up at him with adoration. She marveled at his ability to both keep her interested and keep her wanting more. He said they would walk to dinner, that the restaurant was nearby. With every step she took, she could feel the vibe moving between her legs, the subtle stimulation maker her wetter and wetter with every step. She was also filled with anticipation, wondering when he would turn it on and begin her sweet torture. When they arrived at the restaurant less than ten minutes later, he had not yet turned it on, and suspense was killing her. He didn't turn it on until the waiter came over to drop off the bread and take their drink orders. Micah had his phone out on the table, with the app up and ready to go. As soon as Lana opened her mouth to say that she would have water to drink, she felt the vibe come to life between her legs and her words were cut short by a choked cry that she covered up somewhat convincingly with a cough.

"The lady will have a white wine, and I will have a lager. Thank you very much." As the waiter nodded and walked off, he turned the vibe back off again. "Cat got your tongue there, kitten?" He looked very pleased with himself. She started to reply but again, her words were cut short as the vibe came back, even stronger than before. *This must be level two.* She clenched the table cloth as the strong sensation had her immediately on the verge of an orgasm. Micah took her hand, letting her grip his fingers as hard as she needed to maintain a straight face. Just as she thought she was going to climax in front of all the people sitting around them, he suddenly turned the vibe off again. She sat there panting, feeling her pussy twitch around the vibe, seeking the orgasm it had been building up to. The waiter returned, setting the drinks down on the table.

"Will you need another minute to look at the menu?" Just as the waiter turned his attention to Lana, looking at her expectantly, the vibe came back to life.

"I, I, I," Lana stuttered as if her brain had suddenly been turned off, which is exactly how she felt as her climax came roaring back. She managed to hold it off through sheer willpower alone.

"I think we'll need another minute," Micah interjected and smiled disarmingly at the waiter.

"Ok," he said. "My name is Keith if either of you has any questions." He gave Lana a somewhat quizzical look as he left, but Lana was so lost in her ecstasy that she barely noticed. Micah leaned forward, whispering so that only she could hear.

"Don't hold back, princess. Daddy already told you that you can come as many times as you need to tonight. I know you want to. Go on, let it out." She couldn't hold it in anymore. As her climax shook her body, she bit the palm of her hand, muffling her quiet whimpers as best as she could.

"Good girl. One more, then we can pick what we want to eat for tonight." She looked at him wide-eyed, unable to say a word as he turned the vibe up the third level. Her first orgasm had barely finished when a second one came crashing over her. She was visibly shaking, her eyes rolling back in her head as she twitched and tried not to make any noise. Just when she thought she might lose her mind, lost forever in a swirling vortex of pleasure, he turned the vibe back off. Micah looked at her with a smirk as she sighed and closed her eyes, recovering from her ordeal. He opened his menu and perused it for a moment.

"I think I might have a nice cut of steak tonight, what about you, honey?" he said, his voice dripping with sweetness and innocence. She couldn't answer yet. She was still coming down from the intense sensations he had inflicted on her. It was looking more and more like Micah might be the death of her and she wasn't entirely sure that she minded. With a shaky hand she picked up her menu but the words were a blur. She tried to focus but her mind was still reeling from her orgasms.

"Daddy, you pick something," she said, sighing in defeat. She put the menu down and sat back, closing her eyes.

"Aww, is my baby girl too cum drunk to think straight?" She nodded, too dazed to even be embarrassed. She wasn't sure if she could take it anymore. On the other hand, she wasn't sure that she wanted him to stop, either. She looked around the room, wondering if anyone had noticed or cared about her little "fit." She saw couples and groups of friends all around her, laughing, talking, and eating their meals. The idea that they might look over at any second and see Micah controlling her body was exhilarating. She wanted everyone to know that she was his, and he was hers.

"How does pumpkin ravioli sound, sweetie?" he said sweetly. She braced herself, expecting him to turn the vibe back on as soon as she answered.

"Yes, that sounds delicious." She managed to get out the whole sentence without him triggering the vibe, and she actually found herself missing it.

What is he turning me into? She thought with a smile. He made her feel so wanton and insatiable. Just when she thought she'd had too much, he proved that she hadn't had nearly enough. Micah signaled to the waiter that they were ready to order. As soon as the waiter arrived at their table, the vibe came back to life. Lana's eyes crossed slightly, but she managed to keep a straight face otherwise. Her pussy was incredibly sensitive after her orgasms, but he kept it on the low setting, keeping her warmed up.

"Yes, I was wondering what kinds of seasonings you use on your steaks?" Micah asked the waiter. As the man began to answer, Micah made a subtle movement, and the vibe suddenly started pulsing on and off in an undulating pattern. Their conversation suddenly seemed distant and hazy. As her eyes fluttered closed, the pulse got stronger, keeping the same steady pace.

"My date here is interested in the pumpkin ravioli, but she was wondering if it has any dairy in it," she heard Micah say. He seemed to be deliberately asking unnecessary questions in order to make her cum in front of the waiter. *So evil,* she thought as she gripped the tablecloth and tried not to look like an insane person.

"What do you think, honey. Would you like the ravioli?" He looked at her with fake innocence all over his face, his sea-green eyes twinkling mischievously.

"Mm-hmm," she nodded, and the waiter jotted down her order. He was about to walk off before Micah stopped him, turning the vibe up to the third level, keeping the pulse pattern going. Lana audibly sighed but managed to keep a straight face otherwise. She gripped her legs together, trying to maintain control.

"I was thinking about maybe trying the chicken, what do you recommend?" he asked the waiter, discreetly reprogramming the vibe. He eliminated the pulse, keeping it strong but steady. She wouldn't be able to hold back an orgasm if he kept this up for long. The waiter prattled on about the advantages of one dish over another and Lana could feel her orgasm building, knew it would be long before it came crashing over her and she would be powerless to stop it. Just as she was about to cum, he cut the vibe off. She was left trembling, out of breath, and desperately clenching around the dead vibe, seeking the stimulation that had just been ripped away from her. She glared at him but he pretended not to notice as he handed his menu back to the waiter.

"You know, I think I'll have the steak after all. Thanks so much." He turned back to Lana, grinning like the cat that ate the canary.

"You're so mean," she pouted. Her

breathing was hard as she was still recovering from the intense experience.

"Why would you even say that?" he asked with a fake shocked expression on his face.

"We're having such a lovely evening." She started to reply, but her response was cut short when he turned the vibe back on full force. Before she could even form a thought, she was already cumming again. Her eyes rolled back, and her legs flailed, kicking him under the table. The effort to not make noise was so great that she had to bang on the table a little and hope that people thought that she was laughing. Or killing a bug. She didn't really care anymore, and evidently neither did Micah. He was laughing now and rubbing the sore spot on his shin where she had kicked him.

"I guess I deserved that," he said as he turned the vibe off. Lana relaxed back against her chair, utterly spent. "Had enough, pumpkin?" Lana nodded, still unable to speak. He chuckled and nodded, patting her hand.

"Okay, okay. Daddy will leave you alone for

the rest of dinner. You can relax." Lana took a sip of her wine to soothe her parched throat and steady herself.

True to his word, Micah did not activate her vibe again for the rest of dinner. She scarfed down her ravioli, partially because she was ravenous after cumming so many times and partially because it was incredibly delicious. She was so distracted by the vibrator that she didn't really notice until now how fancy the restaurant he had taken her to was at first. Now that the food was out, however, she was starting to appreciate it more. They ordered dessert, a slice of chocolate cake to share. It was every bit as delicious as the entree had been.

"I can't believe this place is in walking distance to your apartment," she said, taking the last bite of cake. "You must eat here all the time!"

"I did at first but to be honest, these days I just order in from somewhere. I have had a dinner companion as lovely as you in quite some time, and I hate eating alone." She blushed at the compliment and put her fork down.

"Boy, I'm stuffed. As good as that was, I don't think I could eat another bite."

"I'll get the check. Then we can head back to my place." The thought of curling up in Micah's arms and going to sleep sounded really nice. However, something told her he wasn't in the mood for sleep. This suspicion was confirmed when the vibe came back to life when the waiter brought the check. Even on the low setting, it made Lana's eyebrows shoot up and her breath quicken.

"Just a second, if you don't mind," he said to the waiter before he could walk away again.

"I just want to make sure that everything is correct." He pretended to look over the check, but really he was only turning her vibe up another level. Lana had to close her eyes and turn her face down toward her lap to keep from giving the whole thing away. After several long, excruciating seconds, Micah finally handed the check and his card to the waiter.

"Everything looks perfect. Thank you so

much for your patience," he said, giving the man a big smile. He turned back to Lana and smirked. "You have until the waiter to comes back to cum one last time and that will be your last chance for the evening." He turned the vibe up to the third level and watched her face contort, knowing that it would take almost no time at all with the vibes that powerful. Sure enough, her eyes were soon rolling back in her head and she bit her palm again as her body subtly trembled. A tear escaped her eye from the force of her own bite and the force of her orgasm. A low moan escaped her lips but it was too quiet for anyone else but Micah to hear. Micah turned the vibe off as the waiter returned with their check. He signed it with a flourish, being extra generous with the tip just in case the man had noticed anything strange about their dinner out. Lana got up with shaky legs, gratefully taking Micah's arm as he led her out of the restaurant, both of them going slowly until she could regain her footing.

Back at his place, he was on her within seconds of walking in the door. He pushed her roughly over the arm of the couch, forcing her ass in the air and her face down into the cushions. He ripped open the bodysuit and pulled out the vibe, making her moan slightly at the sensation.

"Oh, baby girl, you are so wet right now. You came so hard, didn't you my dirty girl?" She could hear his pants unzipping, and within moments he was inside of her.

"Remember what I said back at the restaurant, no more cumming for the rest of the night." He pumped into her furiously, stroking her butthole with his thumb as he pounded her pussy. He didn't last long, all that teasing back at the restaurant had clearly had an effect on him. He grabbed the flesh of her buttocks as he drove himself deeper inside of her and let loose all the cum that had been building up all evening. It felt so warm and delicious inside of her that she wanted to climax again. She loved the way it felt to be full of his cock and his cum, but she held herself back, priding herself on being a good girl for Daddy. He finally stopped shuddering and twitching inside of her and pulled out, his warm jizz dripping out of her. He sat on the couch and pulled her onto his lap, burying his face in her neck with a shaky sigh. She wrapped her arms around his neck, feeling shaky, exhausted, and completely happy.

"I'm so glad I found you," he whispered, holding her tighter still. "I can't believe how lucky I am, how perfect you are." She smiled dreamily. She had just been thinking the same thing about him.

"So are you, Daddy," she said. They complimented one another so well. She felt certain that fate must have brought them together somehow. As he pulled her face to his for a kiss, she hoped that fate would allow her to keep him, her perfect Daddy.

Chapter 13

Lana navigated her hybrid through the narrow mountain roads. She had grown more accustomed to driving on these steep dirt paths over the past few months, but it still made her nervous. She preferred to let Micah drive when she could, but he wouldn't be able to meet her until later that evening. He had given her the key to his hunting cabin when he saw her last, at Thanksgiving, and asked her if she would spend her Christmas break with him. She had said yes immediately, as if it were even a question. They had spent every moment together that they could over these past few months, visiting each other on holidays, long weekends, even playing hooky a few times in Micah's case. They texted each other and Skyped as much as possible as well, enjoying each other's company just as much as they enjoyed fucking each other. After all of these months together, their passion had not cooled down one little bit. He would often ask her to sneak off to the bathroom to take a sexy picture of herself to send to him. She loved showing off her body to him at every opportunity, never getting tired of how sexy it made her feel. All of the teasing made it so much hotter when they were finally able to get together to relieve the tension. She was looking forward to relieving some of that tension now. Thanksgiving had been fun, but there had been too many family obligations and food comas to fully enjoy one another to the extent that they usually did. That's why they decided to go away for the Christmas break. It was going to be just the two of them for a full week and Lana had been looking forward to this very much.

Micah had to finish up some work stuff before he would be totally free so he had told her to just head straight for the cabin, and he would meet her there later. He gave her a very specific list of instructions to follow once she arrived at the cabin. She loved it when he did that. It could turn the most boring, mundane task into a sexy game. She pulled into the cabin, activating the flashlight on her phone to see in the dark. Letting herself in, she turned on all of the lights and the heat. As she made the place ready, she could feel herself already getting wet, every boring detail suddenly becoming an act of foreplay just because he had ordered her to do it. She lit candles all over the living room, dimmed the lights, and put on the playlist that he had sent to her. Once the cabin had heated up, she stripped off her clothes and hung them carefully in the closet. He liked it when she was neat and tidy, calling her his domesticated little fuckslave. That never failed to make her pussy throb. From her bag, she pulled out the collar that he had bought for her with a heart-shaped lock on the front. Once she put it on, only he had the key to free her again. She fully expected to wear it for the entirety of their stay. Next, she put on a pair of thigh-high stockings, the only clothing that she would be permitted to wear over the next week. The silky material felt wonderful against her bare skin, and she imagined that it was Micah's hand sliding up her legs instead. She checked the time anxiously. It wouldn't be long now. The final touch was a butt plug with a cute furry tail attached. Lana had seen it online and fell in love. Micah had bought it for her as an early Christmas present, having it shipped to her house so that she could wear it this evening. She applied a small amount of lube and slid it in with a quiet squeak. It felt nice, but it would have felt even better if Micah had been the one to slide it in. He would have teased her with it, making her beg for it before finally pushing it in. He knew exactly how to reduce her to a whimpering, horny mess. Once it was in, she checked herself out in the mirror, giving it a little shake. The furry tail danced from side to side, and she giggled. It was every bit as cute as she hoped it would be and the sensations it made as the tail swayed back and forth were very stimulating.

It was almost time for his arrival. She went to the living room and knelt in the middle of the floor, waiting. She kept her knees splayed wide, making sure that he would have full access to every part of her. Her hands were behind her back so that she wouldn't grab for his cock or her clit without permission. He had learned that one of the only effective punishments was to deny her orgasms. Everything else only turned her on and encouraged bad behavior. Denying her the ability to cum, however, kept her in line. A few days without getting off and she became a whiny, needy little thing, willing to comply with whatever he asked of her to be able to cum again. Tonight, he had given her permission to cum as many times as she liked. They had barely gotten to fuck over Thanksgiving, and he said that he wanted to make up for the lost time. However, if she disobeyed him or broke any of the rules, that privilege could be revoked at any time, so she had to be on her best behavior. As she waited, she could feel her skin tingle in anticipation, her pussy already drooling down her legs. At last, she saw his headlights on the wall as he pulled in. As he came inside, her heart leaped with joy. It was finally time.

"Hello, kitten," he said, grinning at her as he took off his coat and put his keys on the hook by the door. He came over to where she knelt, inspecting her from all angles. "Well, don't you look lovely this evening? I love your new tail." He pulled on it lightly, just enough to make her gasp. Then, he kissed her long and deep. She stayed on her knees, mindful that he had not ordered her otherwise just yet, and strained herself upwards to meet his kiss. He broke off the kiss, pushed her gently back down to sit on her heels. As he looked down at her, she noticed that he was still in his suit and the dichotomy of him being fully clothed as she knelt before him, naked and fully on display was deeply erotic. She could his erection already bulging in his pants and licked her lips hungrily. He saw the way she was looking at him and smirked.

"Already hungry for Daddy's cock, little one?" He rubbed it through his pants, teasing her.

"Yes, Daddy. I'm so hungry for your cock. Please, can I taste it?" She looked up at him with her best puppy dog eyes, pleading. He took her by the back of the head and pulled her face to his crotch, rubbing it against his hard cock through the soft fabric of her pants. She moaned as he rubbed himself on her, wanting to taste him all the more as she felt how hard he already was for her. He grabbed her by the hair, forcing her head back so that she was looking up at him. He stroked her face lovingly with the back of his hand as he gazed down at her.

"Unzip my pants, little one," he instructed. She took her hands from behind her back, lowering his zipper slowly while looking up at him. He reached down and freed his erection from her pants, chuckling as the wide eyed expression of glee she got when she saw it.

"Stroke it." She ran her hands up and down the length of him, longing to take him deep down her throat. His hands in her hair kept her firmly in place however and she had to make do with touching it for now. She knew that if she was a good girl for him, her patience would be rewarded.

"Oh baby girl, I've been thinking about this for so long." He took off his belt as she stroked him and let his pants drop. "I've been thinking about your tight little holes and how I'm going to fuck every last one of them. What do you think of that?" She shivered, his dirty words inflaming her desire further.

"Oh, Daddy, yes. Please fuck all of my holes. I need your cock so badly." He smiled and stepped out of his pants, kicking off his shoes.

"Open," he said, and automatically she opened her mouth as wide as she could. He had trained her well over the past few months, and she responded to his commands eagerly and without hesitation. He laid his balls in her mouth, stroking himself slowly as she licked and slurped at him, moaning with excitement.

"That's it, good girl." Finally, he let her taste

his cock, sliding it into her mouth, slowly at first but plunging it deeper and faster with every stroke. He had trained her throat as well, and she could swallow his cock whole without batting an eye now. She was very proud of her deep-throating abilities, loving the way he used her mouth for his pleasure.

"Do you like it when Daddy fucks your pretty little face?" he asked. He loved asking her questions when she had a mouth full of his cock, often saying that she looked "adorable" when she tried to answer him. She made a muffled "yes" noise as he plunged deeper down her throat, moaning with satisfaction.

"Do you want to touch your drippy little pussy?" he asked, continuing to fuck her throat. Again, she answered "yes" as best as she could with his cock lodged in her throat. She didn't move her hand to her pussy just yet. She had learned the hard way that asking her if she wanted something was not the same as giving her permission to do it. He pulled her off of his cock by her hair, letting her gasp for air for a moment, drool dripping from her lips. He looked at her for a moment, enjoying the sight of her as she knelt before him, naked and so eager to please. He plunged back into her throat before finally giving her permission to touch herself. She rubbed at her clit furiously as she choked on his cock, loving the way it intensified every sensation. He groped her tits, pinching the nipples hard as he pumped in and out of her mouth. As he grabbed the back of her head, pushing himself balls deep into her mouth, she came forcefully, her legs jerking underneath her as she finally released the tension that had been building for so long.

"That's it, princess. Good girl," he said as he noticed that she was climaxing. He held her down on his cock until she stopped gyrating, then pulled her up for air. He let her take in a gasp before plunging his tongue in her mouth, tasting her sweet mouth. "Oh, how I've missed you little one." He pushed her back onto her heels, taking his shirt off so that he was now completely naked. He sat down on the couch and started casually stroking his cock as he stared at her.

"Get on all fours," he told her, grinning as she obeyed quickly. "What a good slut. Now turn around and let Daddy see your new tail." She maneuvered herself so that her ass was facing him, letting him get a better look at the butt plug.

"Oh princess, you look so pretty. Do you feel pretty?" She shook her tail and giggled.

"Yes, Daddy, I feel really pretty. Thank you so much for my present."

"You're welcome, baby girl. Now get over here and ride Daddy's cock." She stayed on her hands and knees, knowing how much he liked the way she looked when she crawled towards him. She climbed up onto the couch, straddling him. Her pussy was soaking wet after her orgasm, and he slipped inside of her easily.

"Oh kitten, you're so fucking tight," he growled as he grabbed her hips, holding her down onto his cock. Sometimes, when they were apart, Lana would forget just how big his cock was. As he split her open, stretching her pussy around his thickness, she found herself having to move slowly until she could adjust to his girth. He grabbed her by the face and kissed her deeply, letting her do all the work as she gripped him with her tight pussy. She loved the way he kissed her, slowly and sensually exploring her mouth. She impaled herself on him again and again, loving the way he filled her up.

"Daddy, I missed you so much," she whispered as she slid up and down on him, letting her head fall back in ecstasy. She reached down and touched her clit, working her way toward another orgasm. As she got closer, he began to pump his hips, driving his cock up into her hard and fast. She cried out as she came again, her thighs quivering around him as her eyes rolled back. He let himself go as well, flooding her pussy with his cum as she clenched around him. He pulled her back to him for a kiss, a long slow kiss that contained all of the passion they had been forced by distance to hold back. It felt so good to be in his arms again, to feel him inside of her again. She felt that she had found the place that she belonged with him. They kissed for so long that she felt him begin to get hard again inside of her. Micah had the quickest turnaround time of any man she had ever met. He claimed that it was due entirely to her sexiness, saying that it was only because she drove him so wild. He picked her up, carrying her to the bedroom with her legs wrapped around him, his cock still deep inside of her. They fell onto the bed together, Lana underneath him as they resumed their kiss. She let her fingers run through his silky black hair as their tongues intertwined, and he began to slowly pump himself in and out of her. At last, he was giving her the long slow fucking that they had both been longing for. He put her hand on her clit as he filled her.

"I want you to cum on my cock again, baby girl," he said. He took her nipple in her mouth as she began to rub her button, moaning and squirming beneath him. She spread her legs wider, eager to take him still deeper inside of her. No matter how many time they fucked, it was never enough. He was her sweetest addiction, just as she was his. She let her orgasm build slowly this time, enjoying the feeling of his hands and mouth on her, the feeling of his weight on her, memorizing every detail. She held herself back, wanting to ride the edge as long as possible until she could hold back no longer. She came with a strangled cry, digging her nails into his back as the ecstasy took her.

"Good girl. That's Daddy's good little slut. You're doing so good sweetheart, but Daddy isn't done with you yet." He pulled out, watching with delight as his cum leaked out of her. He maneuvered the butt plug in and out of her, letting his cum and hers lubricate her rear entrance.

"Get on all fours," he commanded. "Daddy wants that ass next." She rolled over, getting up onto her hands and knees. She felt him slide the plug out and place his cock there instead. Slowly, gently, he penetrated her, rubbing her clit as she adjusted to his girth.

"Does that feel good, sweetheart?" he whispered in her ear. She gasped and moaned, struggling to speak through the haze of lust.

"Y-yes Daddy, that is so good. Please fuck my ass, please, please." She was already close to cumming again. She had learned that anal stimulation was a big turn on for her, one of the many things that she had learned about herself since meeting Micah.

"That's it, princess, take that cock." His dirty words pushed her over the edge, and this time as she came, she screamed. So many orgasms so close in a row were bringing her dangerously close to being overstimulated into a whiny, crying mess. As he pumped into her ass even harder, she knew that she would be in that state in very shortly. It was going to be a very long night.

Chapter 14

On Christmas morning, they got up early, excited to exchange gifts. Micah put on a pot of coffee while Lana started a fire. They gave each other their carefully wrapped packages and then tore the wrapping off at the same time. Lana had given Micah a book, the newest in a fantasy series that he was a fan of. Micah had given Lana a box, which she shook curiously.

"Well, go on, open it," he said impatiently. She grinned and took the lid off to see a key laying inside.

"What's this for," she asked, crinkling her brow in confusion.

"It's a key to my apartment. I want you to move in with me, Lana." She looked at him in shock, totally blindsided by the question. "I've already spoken with a friend of mine who works for the Board of Education. He said that they're always in need of good office staff in Atlanta and he can put in a good word for you. What do you think?" She considered it for a moment, wondering what it would be like to be with him all the time, to not have to spend so much time on planes, in cars, on the phone. There was very little keeping her in Jacksonville. She nodded, deciding.

"Okay, I will. I'll move in with you." He let out a whoop of excitement and tackled her, wrapping her up in a bear hug.

"When? When?" he asked excitedly, peppering her forehead with kisses.

"At the end of the year," she giggled, tickled by his excitement. "Let me finish out the year, that will give us plenty of time to make all the necessary arrangements."

"Okay," he grinned. "I suppose I can wait that long." He kissed her, long and deep, then looked her in the eyes.

"I love you, Lana," he said, suddenly very seriously. "I'm so lucky to have you. I don't know what I'd do without you." She grinned, her heart beaming with a happiness beyond anything she had ever felt before.

"I love you too, Daddy. We're both lucky. I don't know what I would do without you either and now we don't ever have to find out."

James's Baby Girls

A romantic DDLG and ABDL love story about a Daddy who trains not one but two baby girls in the DDLG kink

By Tina Moore

Chapter 1

I was the typical track queen in college. I had long blonde hair, big blue eyes, and a smile that never let me down. I was the type of girl who silenced a crowd as I walked past and who was never in short supply of boys who wanted to date me. For those four years at college, my life had been in no uncertain terms, blessed.

Yet, I wasn't at college anymore, and those days of boys waiting in line to date me were long over. The carefree days of college were long behind me as she sat in my office cubicle and looked miserably at the clock on the wall.

At this point, I knew I was dreaming. I didn't work in an office. I worked in a hospital. That was the good thing about lucid dreaming. I could watch myself have an alternative lifestyle but still be able to know what was real and what was just dreaming. I rolled over and smiled as I fell back into the dream.

I had graduated college shortly after an ankle injury and knew how lucky I was to have been given the job I now hated. After having spent four years barely passing my subjects in favor of perfecting my athletic abilities, I was not particularly qualified. Sure, I had my piece of paper saying I had graduated with an arts degree, but I never thought I would actually have to use the degree. But as the doctors confirmed my worst fears, that my running career and Olympic dreams were now out of reach, I had quickly found a job selling life insurance at a big company in the city.

"I need these on my desk by Friday," my boss said as he walked past. He hadn't even bothered to look at me, he never did. I was a long shot from the girl I used to be. No longer did I have an athletic body, I had gained over 20pounds in the five years I had been working at the job. No longer did I have my beautiful long blonde hair and had opted for a short brown bob. I often would look in the mirror and not even recognize the woman staring back at me.

"Sure thing Mr Tims," I replied, trying to smile.

I can't keep feeling this way. I thought to myself as I searched online for a gym.

This might be ok for some women. I honestly don't care how they feel about their bodies. This isn't ok for me. This isn't who I am, I am beautiful, and right now, I couldn't feel less beautiful within myself, I thought booking myself into the afternoon consult.

I didn't think about anything else for the next four hours of my shift. In fact, I was surprised that I didn't think of getting back into shape or even staying in shape sooner.

Maybe I was punishing myself for not going to the Olympics or something, I thought, watching the clock. It was 4:30, and I knew that come 5 o'clock, I would be out of there. No working later tonight, no going to the frozen yogurt store after work today and definitely no medium chips at 7:30 when I was bored with what was on TV. I was determined to get my health back on track.

Five o'clock finally came around, and I lept out of my chair, shut down my computer, and walked out of the office with a confidence I had not felt for years.

Walking down the street, I couldn't help the smile on my face as I walked past people who seemed to get out of my way. Usually, people would frown at me for the space I took, but today felt different. It was as though they knew I was not a person to be messed with, and if I was honest with myself, I had missed that feeling.

I turned the corner and saw the big blue building. I sighed, suddenly feeling overwhelmed by the task I had set for myself. It would be no small feat designing the body I wanted, and I knew that it was going to be hard work.

"Hi, I'm Kelly. I have an appointment with Cleo," I said to the girl behind the desk.

"Hey, um actually, Cleo called in sick about thirty minutes ago. Would you be happy with another trainer, or did you really want her?" The friendly woman behind the counter said.

"Another trainer is fine," I said with a smile. The woman behind the counter typed on her keyboard before looking back up.

"Right, so I've booked you in with Alex. He is really lovely, and here he is. Perfect timing," she said, causing me to turn around.

"Hi," Alex said, reaching out his hand and shaking mine warmly. I smiled at him.

"Let's get this paperwork filled out, and we can talk about what your goals are and such. What do you say?" He asked. I nodded my head and followed him into the office. I sat down, and he gave me a vitamin water and protein ball while I filled out the paperwork and the signing up forms.

"How committed are you to these goals? They are pretty significant," Alex asked, looking at me.

"These last five years have been really tough, and I've really let myself go. I don't want to feel this way anymore. I got a full ride through college because my track performance. I was on target to going to the Olympics, but then I hurt my ankle, and I think I've been punishing myself ever since. Look, this is the girl I really am," I said, taking out my phone and showing Alex the photos of the girl I used to be. He was clearly shocked by the look on his face, and I just gave a half-smile when he looked back at me.

"I'll help you get that girl back. Hell, maybe we even make a new girl because you can't really go backward," he said reaching out to take my hand.

"Can we start tomorrow?" I asked softly. Alex looked at me, the way his eyes sparkled made me feel both nervous and excited.

"Yeah, I think that would be a good idea. Then you can be my project, and I will do anything I want with you," he said, his face going from soft and gentle to angry and dominating as he began disappearing as I fully woke up to a deafening noise in the neighboring apartment.

It was just a dream. He isn't here, and he can't hurt you now, I said to myself. Alex, the man I had worked so hard to forget, still managed to weasel his way into my dreams. I was grateful for the noise. I didn't know what it was or who was doing it. All I knew was, every day, at 7 am, the noise started. Luckily, I had to wake up early most days. It served as an alarm clock, and honestly, it didn't bother me much anymore. I blinked my eyes open, looked at the ceiling and sighed before kicking off the covers. I was a morning person. But today seemed like the kind of day where I could have easily stayed in bed for hours. It was that lonely feeling of waking up all alone, cuddling your pillow at night when you needed extra warmth, and sometimes crying when you needed attention. I mean, I had a lot of friends at the hospital where I worked and even out of it. I made friends with everyone, the other nurses, the doctors, and even some of the patients. I had always just been super friendly like that. But sometimes, the feeling that came with friendship just wasn't enough. I needed something more, and all these acquaintances just weren't cutting it.

I arrived at work just as my shift started and after signing in, headed to get changed. As I was tieing my shoes, my best friend, Thea, walked in and sat down next to me. I was always excited to see her. There was just something about her presence, that made me feel happy. I started bouncing on the balls of my feet.

"Thea," I said, rushing to hug her. With how busy we were, it was surprising to see her at work, so I had to take my chances where I got them. She hugged me and pulled me into her arms. See, this is what I meant. My friends were very affectionate. We loved hugging each other, kissing each other and telling each other, "I love you." But it lacked that thing which only a romantic relationship could bring. It lacked intimacy.

As I melted into her embrace, another nurse came in and kissing me on my cheek, Thea broke our embrace.

"Okay, babes, see you later," I said as I stood and began to walk out of the room.

"Don't forget about tomorrow!" she

exclaimed. I frowned, but I was already out of the changing room and standing in the busy corridor. I didn't want to turn back to ask her what was going to happen the next day. It was going to be Saturday. Nothing exciting ever happened on Saturdays. Except maybe she slept over or something. And since she had a boyfriend, that had become extremely rare. I shook my head and walked away. I figured she was going to tell me after our shift. We always messaged after work. She would tell me the funny or sad things that happened in her day, and I would do the same. She called me her work-wife as I was the only person she would had told all her deepest secrets and fears to. I liked that she felt she could trust me, and over many a bottle of wine, we had watched our friendship grow.

***

The day was a long one, and as I was changing back into my casual clothes, all I wanted to do was go home and sleep. But Thea had other ideas. Apparently, she was coming home with me tonight. She had sent me a message during my shift, asking for me to wait with her by the parking lot. It was in this text she had told me that she was coming home with me.

"Don't tell me you forgot about it?" she asked as soon as she joined me at the parking lot of the hospital. I frowned.

"Forget about what? Can you stop speaking in riddles?" I asked, rolling my eyes. Couldn't she just say it? And stop telling me I had forgotten. I knew I had forgotten. If I hadn't, she wouldn't have been telling me.

"The function, stupid! The function! It's the first one that we were invited to, and you forget?" I widened my eyes. The fact that the function was tomorrow had completely escaped my mind.

"You know I've had a lot on my mind," I said, and she nodded sadly. She wasn't my best friend for nothing. We knew basically everything there was to know about each other.

"It's okay, babes. You'll be fine," Thea said, and I sighed. I didn't respond to that with anything, just walked to my car, and got in.

I turned the radio on loudly so that Thea didn't try to say anything more, and I am glad she took the hint. She was good like that, and I was grateful to have a friend who actually understood me. I also think Thea had realized that her answer had been a little insensitive, especially for someone who had a significant other. I honestly didn't begrudge her, I just hated those *you'll be fine,* and *everything will be okay* answers. After going through a drive-through and getting something to eat, Thea and I reached home. I hated that I was a comfort eater and had ordered two big burgers and a chocolate shake. Tomorrow was going to be a big day. I could feel it.

***

I was not wrong about the day being a big one! Thea and I had gone shopping for the outfits we were going to wear to the function. True to form, Thea had gone for a little black number that hugged all her beautiful curves. It had thin straps at the back and showed off her toned back muscles. She was so beautiful; it was not surprising she never had trouble finding a boyfriend. I had been shopping for three hours by the time I found my dress. I was about to give up and settle for something I already owned when I saw a scarlet red piece of fabric poking out at the back of the store. I walked over and took it down from the hanger. It was stunning, with a low cut V-neckline that I knew would show off my cleavage. I tried it on and looked at myself in the mirror and ran my hands over my curves. It made me feel sexy. It made me feel like a woman, and I knew that a lot of eyes were going to be on me in this dress.

Thea and I took our sweet time getting ready. I wanted to look good. I wanted attention tonight, and I was determined to get it. I showered first, letting the water wash away any insecurity that reared its ugly head. I cleaned, shaved, perfumed, and moisturized my body before leaving the bathroom with just my pink towel wrapped loosely around my toned body. I walked into my bedroom and winked at Thea as she passed me and headed into the bathroom to shower. I waited until I heard the shower water running before I dropped my towel and walked into the kitchen to pour myself a drink. Even if it was just soda, the action of opening a bottle and pouring the contents into a glass was therapeutic. I took a sip and smiled.

Tonight was going to be good. Walking back into my room, I went to my lingerie drawer and ran my hands over the lace material. I selected the panties and a bra in the same color as my dress and smiled as I put it on. I had managed to keep some tan from the summer, and the color made me feel as though I was in Spain all over again. I pulled on my dress just as Thea got out of the shower, and she instinctively came behind me and zipped up the back zipper. Soon enough, she was also ready, and we touched up each other's makeup before kissing the mirror on the way out of the house. We always did this, and the mirror by my front door was covered in different shades of lipstick. Just as I grabbed the front door handle, Thea placed her hand over mine and paused before she repeated what she always did on nights like this one. I sighed and rolled my eyes, knowing what was coming next. I had heard her speech so many times. I could repeat it by heart.

"No drinks from strangers, no rides from strangers..." she started, and I finished "and no kisses from strangers." Maybe it sounded weird, but to us, it wasn't. Thea knew how crazy I could get, especially under the influence of alcohol, even if it was just one glass. I had always been that way, and she had rescued me from myself and the precarious situations I had almost put myself in more times than I could count. That was why I stayed away from alcohol, especially at work functions like the one we were about to be attending. Alcohol and I well, we hated each other.

"We'll have fun, babe," Thea reassured me then placed a kiss on my forehead.

***

We had arrived about ten minutes late, but it wasn't an issue because events like this were always just a loosely timed affair. We entered the function, and I was surprised by how elegantly the venue had been decorated. I liked the music which was playing, and I loved seeing how everyone looked out of scrubs. I had stopped to say hi to everyone I knew then I headed to the bar. I knew the bartender would be shocked when I ordered a plain soda most people usually were, and as my prediction was correct, he looked at me curiously before passing me my drink. I sighed with a feeling somewhere between frustration and loneliness, and walked to a corner of the room and sipped on my drink in the shadows. I was usually more bubbly than this, but all the pointless, empty small talk had taken my spirit away. I was in no mood to do the things I often enjoyed. So I settled for the next best thing. I was watching people doing what I usually enjoyed.

I was watching people when I spotted him. Our eyes met for a while, then someone called for his attention. I sighed a little and let my eyes linger elsewhere, all the while sipping on my soda. Then I started wondering what kind of lives the people in the room lived behind their closed doors. I always enjoyed thinking what kind of dirty things people got up behind their suburban lifestyles. With their tennis on the weekend and country club membership, these were always the most sexually depraved people. Watching them and making up stories about all the filthy things they got up to always brought a smile to my face. For example, the guy with the adorable glasses on his head. He was a lonely doctor, and this was the only time he had to go out. So he took this opportunity thinking it would be nice to socialize with people instead of having another night jerking off alone to an online anime dating site. I wasn't even sure anime dating sites existed, but I figured there'd be something like this on the internet, it was the interest after all.

"Not feeling tonight, are we?" I turned to look at who had rudely interrupted my thought process and saw that it was the man whose eyes I had met when he was on the dance floor. He was even more attractive up close. Then I realized he had asked me a question. I smiled a little sardonically.

"Not really I guess," I replied looking up at him

"This is not your scene?" he asked, and I smiled a little. If only he knew.

"It is. I'm just out of it tonight, I guess," I explained, looking up to meet his beautiful grey eyes.

"Oh. It's one of those nights," he said, and I nodded absently, taking another sip out of my soda. This was weird. Usually, I always had something to say to people. Especially when they were young and hot like the man who was standing next to me. Besides, hadn't I been crying the whole morning about how lonely I was? Why didn't I just take the reins of the conversation and see if the mister was open for dialogue? As I was about to say something, he beat me to it and said, "I'm James. You?"

"I'm Kelly," I said shyly, taking the hand that he had extended. What was happening to me?!

"Beautiful name," James said, smiling. His smile was maybe one of the most beautiful things I had ever seen in my life. It was so beautiful. Fuck.

"Thank you. I'm a nurse at Weiss Memorial. I assume you're a doctor?" I asked, regaining my tempo a little. His serious and grave air just screamed doctor. I could be wrong, though.

"Yes, I am actually. I usually don't attend these... things," James said. Aha. I was right. I couldn't help but laugh at the way he said "things." It was almost like he was physically pained.

"And pray tell, what is wrong with these

things?" I asked, with a small smile at the corner of my lip. I didn't want to pass off as the weirdo who laughed at everything.

"People," he said miserably, and I couldn't help but let out a soft sound. The expression on his face looked too sad to be serious, though, so I laughed.

"And you? Can I ask why tonight is off? Or are you a closet people hater like me?" James asked, and I sighed a little. I debated with myself for some time. For a weird reason, I felt really comfortable with this man that I had just met. So I threw caution to the wind and said, "I'm lonely. And I'm tired of being lonely."

"You don't have any friends?" he asked, and I rolled my eyes.

"That's not what I meant. I mean, I'm tired of searching for a physical and emotional connection with someone. It's exhausting," I mumbled the last part, a little reluctant to look at him now. I had just shared my deepest wishes with a total stranger. He probably thought I was really weird.

"And what if I told you you had found them?" James asked, and I looked up at him sharply. He smiled.

"Let's do this. You give me your number, and we fix up something later on. What do you say?" James asked, smiling like someone who already knew all my secrets.

"Yes," I said timidly, a bit out of character because I was shocked. I definitely hadn't been expecting something like that. I put my number in his phone, and after placing a chaste kiss on my forehead, he walked away with a promise to call me.

"Who was that *hottie*?" Thea asked as she slinked up next to me silently. I was already used to her doing that, so I wasn't startled.

"Guess who just got her number taken by a hot dude?" I fangirled hard, smiling broadly at Thea. She squealed then hugged me

"Fingers crossed bitch," she said.

"Fingers crossed," I reiterated.

***

James and I had certainly made something happen and three months since James and I had been seeing each other. After the night at the function, we were inseparable. We were practically glued to each other on weekends since both of us had full schedules during the week. It was awesome and exciting, and everything that I had spent all that time searching for and I knew that tonight was going to be just as amazing all of the previous evenings together. I knew that I was finally ready for us to take it to the next step. He was coming over for dinner like he did almost every Saturday. But what he didn't know was that this time around, I was dessert. It was the first time that we were going to have sex. I just hadn't been ready before. But tonight, I had planned a whole surprise for him. I just hoped he didn't react negatively.

I was wearing a long t-shirt when he came in. I

didn't want to dress up in anything fancy because I wanted it to be a complete surprise. So I had stayed on the simple side. Dinner had gone well like it always did, with loads of banter and laughter. He made me smile. I just couldn't help it when I was around him.

"Time for dessert," I said, smiling as I came to take his dishes away from the table.

"Babe. I'm stuffed," he said, and I just smiled.

"Trust me. You'll like it," I reassured him, making sure to be a bit cryptic. I went to the kitchen, took off my t-shirt, then lay on the counter.

"Babe," I called out.

"Come to the kitchen," I added. I heard James's footsteps approaching, and I heard his gasp when he saw me lying there with my legs spread wide. I was wearing a matching light pink linger set with my blonde waves tumbling down over my shoulders and nipples.

"Kelly," James started when he was finally

in front of me.

"Won't you kiss me?" I asked. It seemed like that was all he needed, he took me into his arms and kissed me ardently, making up for the other chaste kisses. Without even asking, he led me to the bedroom and lay me on the bed.

"Forgive me, Kelly, this is going to be quick. I've wanted you for way too long," he said, then stripped off quickly. I watched him sheath his dick with a condom he removed from his pocket, and I smiled. He came towards me and kissed me again, this time a little slowly, just as he removed my underwear. I swatted his hands away and removed it myself, marveling in the expression of sheer delight on his face. James took my nipple into his mouth, kneading at the nub with his teeth before sucking at it. I gasped loudly, and it turned into a shaky moan when two of his fingers found my already wet entrance.

"You're ready for me already, aren't you, princess?" He asked. I preened at the name and gasped out.

"Yes, Daddy," I moaned as James removed his fingers and positioned himself at my entrance, slowly working his way to the hilt. He started out slowly. Then he started thrusting fast, causing my breath to come out in gasps.

"Yes, Daddy. Right there, Daddy," I screamed at the top of my voice as he continued pistoning his dick in and out of my wet hole.

"I'm cumming," I screamed suddenly and wrapped my legs around his waist. A few seconds later, James let out a loud grunt then went limp on top of me.

"Daddy?" I called out. When he didn't respond, I said, "James. Are you listening?"

"Why do you call me, Daddy? Is that some sort of kink?" James asked, after rolling off me. I was silent for some time. I knew this was going to come. I didn't know how to explain it. I didn't want him to be disgusted by me. I bit my lip. Then said a little shyly, "I want you to be my Daddy."

"What exactly do you mean by Daddy?" he asked, looking at me intently. I grew stupidly shy for some reason, so I put down my head. I didn't know how exactly to explain. The words were there, but I was scared to speak because I was in little space. I didn't want to scare him.

"I– Do you know about DDLG?" I asked, enunciating my words slowly so as not to go into little mode.

"I.. I want us to have that. I want you to be my Daddy." I watched him frown a little, then he said, "Can I think about all this?" He asked, clearing his throat. I knew he wasn't going to accept it immediately, but it kind of hurt.

"Okay," I said plainly and turned away. I heard James sigh, then he dressed up, placed a kiss on my forehead, and left.

Chapter 2

James's POV

After I left Kelly, I sat in my car, debating with myself. I didn't know whether to go back to her or just to go home. I finally decided to go home, and I felt like such an asshole. I felt overwhelmed. And I wasn't even sure that this was the right word for it. Kelly had been so sweet. Having her was one of the best things ever. But then she said she was a little. What was that even? And her calling me Daddy? I wasn't too sure if I actually liked it. There could be a lot of things behind the name. And I honestly wasn't sure that I wanted to analyze that. I didn't know how all this made me feel. I hated the fact that I was so weak that I had left Kelly all alone, after sex, vulnerable. But I also didn't want to give her the wrong idea. What if I didn't want this "Daddy" thing? What if I didn't want to be her Daddy? Staying there was just going to hurt us both more.

I sighed and shifted in my bed. Not only were my balls blue, but my heart also was heavy, and my mind was racing. I wanted to be it for Kelly. But I wasn't ready to accept how the whole thing had made me feel. I sighed and picked up the phone. I knew that she was probably not asleep, so I called her. She picked at the first ring.

"Da– James?" Kelly answered, and my heart warmed up. Kelly was the only person that had succeeded in making me feel this way. I mean, I was 37, the future was all that mattered to me. And I didn't want Kelly's and my future put in peril when we had barely even started.

"Baby girl," I said, wishing that I had not stupidly left.

"I'm sorry for leaving so abruptly," I said and waited for her to reply.

"I– does this mean you're going to come back?" Kelly's voice was hopeful, and I felt bad that

I might break her heart.

"I probably shouldn't be saying this, but you're the only person that I want to be my Daddy. James, you're the only person who makes me feel this way. I feel like I can be myself with you. I feel so... loved when I'm with you," Kelly said. I frowned a little. Kelly sounded so vulnerable that I felt like I should go back to her.

"We'll talk about it tomorrow, okay? I'll come over, and we'll talk about it. For now, I want to sleep. Close your eyes. Go to sleep." I said to her, hoping that it would make her feel better.

"Will you stay on the phone with me, James?" Kelly asked innocently, and I shifted uncomfortably in my bed.

"Yes, baby girl, I will. Be a good girl and sleep now," I said, trying to comfort her.

"I love you, Daddy. Goodnight," she replied, making me smile.

"I love you, princess. Sleep tight," I said but stayed on the line until I heard her breathing even out. I felt less guilty now. And I knew that if I hadn't called, she would have spent the whole night agonizing. Now that that was done, maybe it was time for me to sleep as well.

I tried for a couple of minutes, but I just couldn't find a position that was comfortable enough. So I gave up on it. I stared up at the ceiling for some time. Was it wrong that I wasn't ready yet to come to terms with my feelings concerning all this? The Daddy thing and all? All I knew was that Kelly calling me, Daddy, made me feel good about myself. But I didn't want us to rush into something that we weren't ready for. Especially since I didn't have any single notion about this lifestyle.

Yes, she called me Daddy. So what? I thought to myself as I got out of bed and walked to my computer. While it was powering on, I stretched a little and stared into space. I rarely felt out of depth. But right now, without even knowing what I was contemplating getting into, I felt that way. After signing in, I pulled up a tab. And wrote DDLG in the search bar. Just then, I heard a ping sound from my phone. I picked it up and frowned when I saw a message from Kelly. She was supposed to be asleep. The message was just a couple of site links signed with her name and a love emoji. I smiled in spite of myself.

Thank you, princess, now go to bed. Was the message I replied to her with. Without waiting for a response from her, I opened up one of the site links she had sent to me. I took a deep breath and started reading intently, trying not to miss out on any detail.

DD/LG, an acronym for Daddy Dominant/Little Girl in its core, is a kinky age-play/role-play between two consenting adults. I frowned a little then continued scrolling. I wasn't turned off or disgusted, just intrigued. Maybe the disgust was going to come as I read further, but for now, I wanted to know more. All the notions that I had had about the lifestyle were getting dispelled. I didn't know what I was expecting to fall on– some kind of weird incestuous roleplay maybe– but this site specifically stated that there was nothing incestuous about DD/LG. It also stated that the

Daddy Dom was the caregiver, and he dominated and disciplined the little while the Little Girl took on a child-like role of a sweet girl, and she regressed in age. A lot of things made sense when I read that. Kelly was often very child-like in her behavior. But I had thought nothing about it, believing that it was in her nature to be that way. Knowing this about her felt comforting. It was hard to imagine how much she had restrained herself with me simply because she didn't want to make me feel uncomfortable. I continued with my reading, marveling at just how many signs I had missed when it came to Kelly. I felt extremely insensitive. And I didn't think anything would help to stop making me feel that way.

I stared blankly at the screen on my phone. After a moment of indecision, I closed up the tab. Kelly and I were going to talk more tomorrow, and we were going to discuss all this. Maybe I was just being a horny old bastard, but the thought of everything about this lifestyle interested me. I got back into bed and stared at the ceiling for a while, a hundred and one thoughts on my mind. I wasn't exactly sure about what I was going to tell Kelly tomorrow. But I had some feeling that it was going to go well. And with thoughts of all that on my mind, I drifted off to sleep.

***

The next morning being a weekend, I woke up pretty early. I had been a practicing doctor for years. Waking up early was a routine for me. Besides, I worked out on weekends, so I needed to be up early. After a hardcore weights workout and a shower, I headed towards Kelly's place. I thought of what to say to her. I didn't know if I should listen to her opinion first before agreeing to anything. I didn't want to raise her hopes high then shatter them. I sighed and parked my car. Granted, all this interested me. I was curious. And it was something I would love to try. But I didn't want my curiosity to end up hurting Kelly. Hurting her was the last thing on my mind. And that was why I wanted us to talk before setting up anything with each other.

I went to her apartment and tried the door. It was open, so I went in, frowning. I had told Kelly numerous times to stop leaving her door open. She was a very beautiful woman. And if anybody with wrong intentions found out that she never locked her door, they might hurt her. I walked in and sighed when I saw that she wasn't even in the living room.

"Kelly?" I called out, removing my coat and hanging it up. It wasn't too chilly outside but cold enough that I needed to wear a coat. This was my favorite type of weather.

"In the bedroom James," she called out. I walked towards the bedroom, and when I reached the door, I started.

"Kelly, how many times have I told you to lock the door? What if an intruder–" words suddenly escaped me. Kelly was standing in front of the mirror, looking completely different from what I was used to. She had her hair up in pigtails.

She was wearing an oversized t-shirt which reached her mid-thigh and a pair of thigh-length socks.

"Hi, Daddy. Do you like my outfit?" she asked, smiling cutely at me. I did actually. It was different from what I was expecting to see her in, the usual shorts and cami she wore at home, but I liked it. I held out my hand, and she took it, then we walked to the living room.

"Have you had breakfast?" I asked, pausing a little.

"No, Daddy. I was waiting for you," she said shyly, and I smiled. The fact that she needed me it made me feel powerful and important. It made me feel good, and it made me want to treat her like the princess she was. I was beginning to get with the whole dynamic of this lifestyle. I had forgotten all about the fact that I had had doubts the whole drive over. Seeing Kelly made me happy. Hearing her call me, Daddy, was a special kind of feeling. I wanted to be needed by Kelly. It was a weird realization. But it was true nonetheless.

"Okay, come along. We'll make omelets. You can help me chop up–" Kelly's laugh interrupted me. It was weird how I had heard her laugh before, but this was different. It sounded like she wasn't holding anything back. And I guess she really wasn't. I liked that she felt she could trust me with this part of herself. I guess some other people would freak out, even more than I had.

"James, I can't be anywhere near a knife. Silly daddy," she said. It was so difficult to associate the vulnerable and sad Kelly to the one who was standing in front of me right now. She looked vibrant, happy, and playful.

"Oh," I said, and she nodded.

"Okay, then you can watch me while I cook, and we'll talk more about this whole thing. How does that sound?" I asked.

"Yes... Daddy, does this mean you are going to be my Daddy? Officially?"

"Yes," I said, beaming despite myself. I couldn't believe how, in just a few short hours, my whole world had turned completely upside down, and I liked it. I saw her eyes get misty, and she hugged me. I held her tight and just enjoyed the feeling of her being in my arms.

"I love you, Daddy. Thank you for agreeing to be my Daddy. I won't ever do anything to displease you. I'll be a good little, I swear. The best little on Earth," she rambled on, and I frowned a little. Looks like someone had hurt my baby girl in the past before.

"We are all humans Kelly. We make mistakes from time to time. And as for agreeing to be your Daddy, I don't regret it. And I won't," I said firmly, as I saw that she was about to protest. I placed a kiss on her forehead and smoothed her hair. Kelly smiled shyly and buried her head in my chest. Then she stood on tippy toes and placed a soft kiss on my mouth. I smiled.

"Now, let's get this breakfast going, shall we?" I asked rhetorically, carrying her up bridal style into the kitchen. Kelly let out a loud squeal, and I laughed. I couldn't help but have this anxious feeling at the back of my mind, though.

"Kelly?" I called, and she answered absently.

"Did someone hurt you in the past?" I asked, then mentally face palmed myself, disappointed at how insensitive I sounded. I watched as her face shuttered, and I immediately regretted my question.

"Can– can we talk about something else?" she asked. I nodded, then watched her for a moment. I wanted her to open up to me. But I knew I hadn't earned it yet. Until then, I was going to treat her like a queen, just like she deserved.

Kelly's POV

I was lying in James's lap, watching the ceiling. I honestly couldn't explain the feeling that had taken over me when he had said he would be my Daddy. I felt like crying with relief and laughing with joy at the same time. When he had left me all alone after we had sex and after I told him I was a little, I felt so brokenhearted and thought I was going to die. I couldn't even cry. I just felt really empty. When he had called me, though, I didn't want to get too hopeful. His voice had soothed me, even though he technically wasn't giving me what I needed. I didn't know how to explain it, but at that moment, I felt like he needed a push. Maybe I was too forward, but I had gone ahead and sent him links. It worked out eventually, so I didn't regret anything, I guess. And him coming to me the day after to reassure me. It made me feel safe. It made me feel like I was something worth keeping. I felt loved. I felt special.

"James?" I called out.

"Hmm?" James answered, and I smiled. The happiness that came over me every time he answered to me wasn't really something I could explain. It was like I had bared some parts of myself to him, and he hadn't run away or anything. I just felt like jumping on him and screaming to the whole world that he was *my* Daddy, and nobody could take him away from me.

"I just felt like calling you," I said shyly, then

buried my head in his chest and inhaled his scent deeply. I honestly didn't know how I was going to survive being apart from him... I really hoped that he stayed with me forever. I knew it was childish of me to have such fairytale thoughts. But it was honestly having them that kept me going. James laughed, and his chest rumbled. It was a nice feeling.

"Baby girl," he called.

"Yes, James," I answered dutifully.

"Sit up now. Let's talk. About all this," he said, and I lifted my head from his chest to look at him. It was interesting how his expressions could change so quickly. From smiling to looking extremely serious.

"Okay, Daddy," I said, but I didn't leave his lap. It was the most comfortable place in the world for me at that moment.

"We need to discuss the whole dynamics of this. The rules. And everything. Don't you think?" James asked, and I nodded dutifully. I knew he needed to put some rules up in place. And I also knew he wasn't too familiar with all this, so I was going to try my best to help him out.

"Okay, we will start with the rules. Rule number–" James began to say.

"Wait for Daddy," I exclaimed excitedly, with a huge smile on my face. The stern look on his face, though, made me quiet down.

"Rule number one, don't interrupt Daddy when he's speaking. We'll let it slide for now. But don't do that again, princess, okay?" He warned with a kiss on my cheek.

"Yes, Daddy," I replied, snuggling into him. There was some silence for a while, and the gloomy look appeared on his face again. Did this mean he no longer wanted to be my Daddy? Was he going to let me go?

"Are you mad at me, Daddy?" I asked in a small voice, not even bearing to look up at his face.

"I'm not mad, Princess. Just thinking," he responded, and I let out a sigh of relief. I lay my head on his chest again and let out another sigh.

"Can we go on with the rules, Daddy?" I

said, my voice a little muffled. He was silent again, and I frowned.

"James?" I asked cautiously.

"Don't you think we should talk about all this before getting into the rules?" he asked, and I frowned. I knew exactly what he was hinting at, but I didn't want to give anything away.

"Talk about what?" I asked, pretending not to understand.

"Talk about us. Talk about each other. I don't want this to be an empty relationship with just sex, and you calling me Daddy." I nodded. It was understandable. I knew that sooner or later, I was going to bring up my past. And we had been seeing each other for three months! I felt so comfortable with him, and I genuinely meant it when I said I loved him, but I didn't know if I could talk about what happened.

"Don't shut me out, baby girl. That won't work anymore. Look at me," James said, and I looked up at him. He was right about me shutting him out. I did that often. James placed his hands on both my cheeks and said, "I'm here. I'm going to listen when you're ready. If you don't feel ready, you don't have to say anything, okay?" James explained. I nodded and closed my eyes. I appreciated this man.

"How do you feel about shopping?" James asked, and I perked up.

"I love it!" I exclaimed. It was one of the things that I didn't often do, but it has this therapeutic effect when I do.

"Are you going dressed like that, or do you want to change?" He asked. I paused to look at myself self consciously after James asked that question.

"Do you want me to change? I don't want to embarrass you or anything," I said, scratching at my arm.

"You look beautiful. And you'd never embarrass me," he said and placed a kiss on my forehead. I smiled up at him. It was scary how quickly my walls could fall with James.

Chapter 3

It had been a week since James and I had had sex, and I had confessed to him about me being a little. The week had been pretty fun, with us sneaking as much as we could afford after work, which was very hard. He had spent some nights over at my place, and I was always sad when his beeper had to ring. But it was Saturday again, and hopefully, we were going to spend the whole day together. Without any distractions. I had packed a couple of clothes, and I waited patiently for him to come to pick me up. It was weird just how quickly I was getting really attached to him. But then again, that's how I was.

"Kelly?" James called as he walked into the room. I smiled at him brightly. I stood up and launched myself into his arms, and I felt him laughing.

"Why are you acting like we didn't see each other in years?" James asked, and I blushed a little.

Did that mean he didn't miss me? I anxiously thought to myself.

"I.. I just missed you. You didn't miss me?" I asked, rubbing at my arm. I hated when this insecure side of me came out.

"Come here. I missed you," James said making me smile. It felt nice to be appreciated.

"Are you all packed up? Can we leave now?" James asked, and I nodded, standing away from him and rocking on the balls of my feet. I pointed to my bag when he raised a brow. He picked it up and tapped my right butt cheek, and I blushed. We got out, and I locked the door up. We walked to his car in silence. I had so many questions, but I didn't want to annoy him by asking all of them, so I kept quiet. The drive was silent, as well. James kept sneaking looks at me as if he expected me to burst into chatter at any moment. It was the first time I was going over to his place, and I was nervous. When I get nervous, I say stupid shit, so I preferred to keep my mouth shut.

"Why are you so quiet?" James asked, and I blushed a little.

"I don't know.. I'm just nervous," I confided in a small voice. I looked away, then I felt his hand on my lap, stroking it softly.

"You have no reason to be," he said, and I sighed deeply. I knew this. But I couldn't help being paranoid. I was too scared to lose him because of my past. And I couldn't even tell him that because I had been too scared last night to tell him about my past.

"I know. I just..." I sighed again. Then brightened up a little and asked, "What do you have planned?" I asked with a small smile.

"It baffles just how quickly you can bounce back up. I love it," he said, completely avoiding my question. Nevertheless, I blushed at the kind compliment.

"You didn't answer my question," I said, and James laughed.

"It's a surprise," he said and took my hand

into his and kissed it. I felt like melting at that instant. This man was everything.

I stayed quiet for the rest of the ride, enjoying the feeling of my hand in his. We reached soon enough, and James opened the door for me. Apparently, I wasn't allowed to. I didn't mind in the slightest, though. It made me feel like a princess. And I told him this.

"You're my princess," James said and placed a kiss on my lips. I sighed when he ended it. Since last week, we hadn't had sex again, no matter how much I had tried to seduce him. I tried not to think about it too much. But I hoped it was going to change this weekend. We got into James' house. It was huge, and I wondered how he's been surviving living there all alone.

"How don't you feel lonely living here all alone?" I asked, looking up at him as he held my hand and led me to the bedroom.

"I'm used to it. And you're here now, aren't you?" he asked with a tiny smile. I blushed and grinned widely at him, preferring not to say anything. We got to the bedroom, and when he opened it, I was in awe. His bedroom was big. But that was not what made me happy. In the middle of the room, there was a big bed, and it was filled with all the things a little might need. I turned towards him and looked up with a pleading look on my face.

"Can I Daddy?" I asked, itching to go there already.

"Yes," was all James had to say before I ran there. There were diapers, pacifiers, stuffies, blankies, and so much more. It was like a little heaven. I refrained myself from jumping on the bed, though, tapping my toes until Daddy authorized me to move.

"You don't like them?" his voice came from behind me, and I shook, startled.

"I do, Daddy," I answered, swaying from left to right.

"Then what are you waiting for? You don't want to play with your toys?" He asked, and I smiled big. I placed a kiss on his mouth, then ran to the bed and jumped into it. I picked up one of the stuffies and hugged it to my chest, then dropped it and picked another one. I jumped up excitedly and skipped to Daddy. I placed a kiss on his mouth that he deepened. I sighed when the kiss ended.

"You're the best, Daddy," I said, and I felt his arms tighten around me.

"Now let's change," Daddy said, and I jumped up excitedly. I watched as Daddy packed the things he had gotten me neatly, then he selected a pink onesie from the pile of dresses. He beckoned me to him, and I went obediently. I was wearing a simple t-shirt, jeans and I had already removed my boots. He undressed me gently, stopping once in a while to place kisses on random parts of my body, on my collarbone, on my calf, on my shoulder. At this point, I wanted to just jump into his arms and beg him to take me.

"Lay in my lap, let me put your diaper on," he commanded, and I obeyed. At this point, he could have said, go and fall in the Atlantic and I would have. James spread my legs gently, and I moaned.

"Someone's wet, huh," he said, and I squirmed. I gasped when I felt his fingers parting my pussy lips.

"Daddy," I moaned out as he rubbed my clit.

"You like that?" he asked, and I gasped. One hand was rubbing my clit, and the other was circling my wet hole. I could feel my juices running down my thigh.

"Yes, Daddy, I love it," I gasped out.

"Please, Daddy," I said, unable to bear any more of his teasing. He slid one finger into my wetness, and I sighed deeply. His thrusting was slow at first. Then he added a finger. I let out a gasp. He was still thrusting slowly, and I was rocking my hips to meet his fingers.

"Daddy," I whined, then he added a finger and started thrusting in earnest. It was like he had transported me to seventh heaven. The room was silent, and the only thing you could hear was my loud pants.

"You like that baby girl? Tell me how you

like it. I can feel your hole clenching around my fingers," Daddy rasped out, and I moaned.

"I love it, Daddy. Yes, Daddy, right there!" I screamed and clenched my fists tight as the waves of the orgasm crashed over me. I felt his hands on my shoulders, and he made me sit up. I was straddling his laps, and I reached for his zipper. I opened it and removed his already straining erection. I stroked it a little then guided it into my wetness. Both of us sighed as he got into the hilt.

"Ride me, princess," Daddy rasped out. I reached out and held his shoulders, gasping as he bent and took a nipple into his mouth.

"Daddy," I breathed out, rocking my hips slowly at first, then leaning against his chest and moving in up and down movements. Daddy took hold of my face and kissed me. Both of us abandoning all the passion we felt for each other in the kiss. I gasped into the kiss and dug my fingers into his shoulders as a quick orgasm came over me. I felt Daddy jerk into me a few times, then he stilled. We stayed there for a while, him in me, my head on his shoulders. Then he spoke.

"Come, we'll take a bath. Then we'll go over the rules. Deal?" I nodded. I was too tired to argue anyway.

***

"Baby girl?" I heard. I opened my eyes groggily and saw Daddy standing over me. I had probably fallen asleep after the bath. I was dressed, though. The feel of the diaper against my bottom was comforting. It wasn't something I had thought I'd ever feel again.

"Come on. We have to go through the rules now," he said, and I rubbed my eyes sleepily. I sat up and watched him open his drawer. He removed a slightly thick pile of papers, and I widened my eyes.

"Are you hungry?" he asked, and after thinking for a while, I nodded. Daddy came with a feeding bottle and sat me in his lap. I stared up at him as he fed me, wondering what I had done to deserve such a loving Daddy. When I was done, he removed the bottle and wiped my mouth. We settled in, and he picked up what I presumed was the rules and contract.

"Daddy, are we going to read all this?" I asked in surprise. I really didn't want to.

"I want you to read all of it. I'll give you time to do that obviously. And when you're done, you tell me what you don't agree with. Deal?" Daddy said, and I sighed a little.

"You'll stay here with me, won't you, Daddy?" I asked, looking up at him with a pleading expression on my face. I smiled when he nodded, and I opened the first page. It was written boldly, OUR DDLG RELATIONSHIP. I started reading, and most of it was just explaining what everything meant. I smiled. Daddy had done a lot of research to make sure everything went well. I continued reading. Then I looked up at him.

"Daddy, I have an issue," I said, and he came to my side.

"What's that, baby girl?" Daddy asked,

looking down at the contract.

"The duration.. it says 'indefinite' instead of 'forever,'" I said, then stuck out my tongue to make it known I was joking. He laughed and sat behind, pulling me into his chest. I kept on reading, paying more attention when I reached the rules I was supposed to follow. They were pretty easy.

Rules

1. No cussing

2. Always talk to Daddy if there's something wrong

3. Before making purchases that aren't really essential, check-in with Daddy

4. Never lie to Daddy

5. Be polite and respectful to everyone, especially Daddy.

6. Get at least six hours of sleep every night

7. Respect each rule, or you'll get punished

8. Don't touch yourself without Daddy's permission

9. If you break a rule, tell Daddy

I was okay with these rules. So I looked up at Daddy.

"Where do I sign Daddy?" I asked, looking up at him.

"Are you sure there's nothing you'd like to change, baby girl?" he asked, and I shook my head. I trusted Daddy. Maybe not as much as he would love me too. I took the pen he stretched at me and signed. When he took everything from me, I sat up suddenly. I had forgotten to talk to him about something! Mostly because I wasn't very sure that he was going to accept to be my Daddy.

"Daddy?" I called, and he let out a grunt in response.

"Well, there's this kink party next week. I was wondering if you'd like to go with me?" I asked, hoping he would say yes. I closed my eyes and waited for his response. I really didn't want to hear a no.

"Sure, baby girl. When is it?" He asked.

"Next weekend, Daddy," I replied.

"You really want to go?" James asked, and I

nodded frantically.

"Alright then, Princess." I squealed excitedly and kissed him.

"You won't regret it, Daddy," I assured him. It was going to be fun. It was on Saturday. Daddy and I reached the venue a little late. But that was because my diaper had gotten wet and he had to change it. But it wasn't really a problem. I just wanted to have some fun with James. As soon as we got in, I spotted most of my friends sitting in one corner, and I fought the urge to squeal. I hadn't seen any of them in a while since I didn't have anyone to be my Daddy. Daddy walked us up to a group of where Daddies were sitting. I knew all of them, but I was shy. I looked down and stood behind Daddy partially. I didn't really want to be the center of attention.

"Are you with Kelly?" one of them asked, and I blushed. The blushed intensified even more when Daddy affirmed this.

"Sure do hope you treat her right after what that bastard did to her." One of the other men said.

Daddy and I tensed at the same time. But he didn't ask them any questions, and I was grateful for that. I wanted to tell him myself. I turned towards my friends and saw some of them waving at me. I squealed and hid my face behind James's back.

"Do you want to go play with your friends Kelly?" Daddy asked, and I nodded frantically.

"Go ahead," he said, and I skipped off.

"Is that your new Daddy?" Reese, one of my friends asked.

"Yes," I responded shyly, "He's the best Daddy ever."

"Is he better than you know who?" Reese asked again, and I nodded. My previous Daddy had been a horrible person. But James was nothing like that. At that, all of us turned towards our Daddies and watched them. They seemed to be in an engaging conversation. So we turned back to each other and started talking.

"Oh my God, my Daddy punished me in public, and I really liked it," Francie, one of my louder friends said after a while of us discussing, and we all gasped. All of a sudden, I wanted that. I wanted Daddy to punish me.

***

"Daddy, I'm home!" I call from the front door. When I got home from work and saw James's car in the driveway, I was so excited that he was home early, I ran up the garden path and quickly opened the door. But I knew he wouldn't have heard me come in because I heard the shower running. I put my bag down on my special pink bag hook in his mudroom and kicked my wet boots off, placing them on the shoe rack just the way he liked. I like that I can do the things that Daddy taught me without him needing to remind me to do them. Sometimes I really love being his good girl, today felt like one of those days. I giggle as I tiptoe to the bathroom, hearing him singing in the shower. I've never had a Daddy who sings in the shower before, and I sit by the door and listen to his songs. James is a surprisingly good singer. I was surprised when he first sang for me in the car ride home from our first picnic in the woods. I had pressed the window down, my hair getting windswept as I felt the air against my face, and he turned the radio down and began to sing. His song, making me blush and unsure of what to do as I sat quietly in my seat and listened. He looked at me several times during it, making me uncertain of what to say, so I just settled in and let him reach me with his song. I've gotten used to him suddenly bursting out in song since then.

I've even found myself missing it when he's had a big day and doesn't have a song in his heart.

"Oh, little girl, I didn't hear you come in," James says opening the door suddenly. I giggle, and he bends down to kiss me before taking my hand and leading me to the bedroom.

"How was your day?" He asks, making me roll my eyes. I hate talking about my day with anyone else but Thea. Especially with doctors. They think they are the most important people at the hospital, and even though James isn't like that, I'd rather not talk about my day with him.

"Lame," I reply, not interested in telling him about my boring day filled with boring people who lead boring lives. He smiles, and I can see he has other things on his mind as well.

"Why don't you come here," he says, patting his lap as he sits down on the edge of the bed. I bite my bottom lip, surprised that he'd want to give me a random spanking but move to him as instructed. I hold my breath as I lay across his lap.

"Lift up your skirt," James whispers, making my heart race as I reach behind and expose my emerald green lace thong. I can tell he likes it by the way his hands move over my firm, full ass, feeling my wetness as he pushes my thighs apart.

"Such a pretty little girl," he says, patting my ass. James holds my head in the nook of his arm as I tense my thighs on his lap and fight my urge to snuggle into him. I know that he isn't finished with his fun by the way he is running his finger up and down my wet, panty-covered slit. I suck my bottom lip, only for him to replace it with his thumb, correcting me when I slowly stink my teeth into it for fun.

"If you have too much energy, I'll give you something else to do," he says, making me try to hide my smirk. He pulls my panties to the side and continues his slow onslaught, making me whimper in frustration. He was waiting for that. I know how he likes me on edge, begging for his touch.

"No, you're not there yet," he casually says, continuing to tease me. I want to have more of him, as I slightly buck my hips, wanting him inside of me.

"Don't be such a slut. You'll get what I give you," he says, making me groan in frustration. Suddenly, he enters me with two fingers, curling them inside of me and stroking up and down my arching back.

"My little gymnast," he says as I stuck on his thumb and push my hips down on his hand.

"Come on, then, come and get it," he says, taking his thumb from my mouth and wrapping his arm around my neck as he pushes into me firmly, making me take him hard and fast.

"Don't make me wait," he whispers. I know what I'm supposed to do as I begin backing up onto his hand, grinding down on the fingers he has filled me with as his thumb begins to rub my clit, making me moan.

"Good girl," he says, standing up and watching as I catch myself before I hit the ground.

"Just like a little pussy cat," James says, watching as my body contorts, the muscles of my toned arms, tummy, and thighs flexing in the subtle light coming from that hallway lamp. I move to stand in front of him, unsure of what he wants me to do before he smiles and reaches out for my hand, pulling me to him.

Chapter 4

James's POV

Kelly woke me up with her screams. I took her into my arms and soothed her until she woke up. Then I frowned. She looked really scared, and the tears on her cheeks told me this was really bad.

"Hey, baby. Want to talk about it?" I asked, smoothing her hair down. Last night at the kink party had gone so well. Kelly had behaved decently, and I had made new friends that were also into this lifestyle. So I didn't understand what had provoked the nightmare and screaming.

"I. No. Yes, Daddy. Please," Kelly said, and I sat up completely in bed.

"Wait, before that. Let's check your diaper," I said, and she laid her face down with her butt facing me. I opened up her onesie, and when I checked her diaper, it was still dry. I buttoned up the onesie again and sat her up again.

"Ready to talk now?" I asked, and Kelly nodded. After some silence, she started, "I had a Daddy before you. His name was Alex. I met him when I was 20, and he introduced me to this lifestyle. We were together for three years." I watched her as she spoke, wishing I could take all the pain from her little body. She continued, "He was good to me at first. He was really caring and had my best interests at heart. I really loved him. And I thought he loved me too." I clenched my palms at the thought of her loving someone else, but I didn't interrupt Kelly. I could tell from her demeanor that she really needed to pour out everything.

"Then he became really controlling, way more than a Daddy should. He would try to stop me from going to the hospital and punish me each time I had a night shift even though it wasn't my fault." I fought the urge to punch something. So I just took Kelly's face into my hands and placed a soft kiss on her forehead, then urged her to continue.

"He would stop me from doing things, from seeing my friends. We stopped going to kink parties together, and he basically cut me off from the rest of the world. And he kept on reminding me that I was useless and that he was the only Daddy in the world who could tolerate me. Because I was such a bad little.

"He would play with my feelings. Bring other littles home and play with them in front of me. He wanted to break me, and he was succeeding slowly. Then the beatings started. They were no longer punishments. I had bruises everywhere, and I became ashamed of my body and wore heavy makeup and clothes to cover my whole body. My friends grew worried about me. And Kyle, who is a police officer, was able to get me away from him. I filed a restraining order against him, and I've never seen him since then," Kelly explained to me. I was sure I looked distraught at hearing the life she had lived in the past.

It was silent, then I asked, trying to control the barely restrained fury that was begging to come out, "Is that what made you have the nightmare?"

"Yes, Daddy. I dreamt that he came back and that he hurt you really bad," Kelly said and started sobbing. I pulled her into my arms and placed kisses everywhere I could reach while whispering reassurance into her ears. When the sobs subsided, I lifted her face and said seriously, "Princess, you are more than enough. You are one of best things that has ever happened to me, and I wouldn't trade you for anything in this world. And don't worry, that dickhead is part of the past, and he will remain there, okay?" I said seriously. Kelly nodded, then leaned forward and placed a kiss on my lips.

"I love you, Daddy," she said.

"I love you too, princess. Now let's go to sleep," I said and placed one last kiss on her forehead. I had a hard time falling asleep because of all the pent up rage. I hated men like that, ones who used their power to prey on others, especially the women they were supposed to protect. I looked at Kelly, who had already fallen asleep, and I placed a kiss on her lips and tried to fall asleep as well.

***

A week later, I went over to Kelly's place. I was really contemplating asking her to move in with me, and it would make things way easier, but I was scared she was going to think everything was going too quick. And I honestly wasn't sure I was ready either. I got into her apartment as her door was still unlocked. I walked into her bedroom, preparing to scold her, but she hid something from me and looked at me with a defiant look on her face. Okay this was definitely not what I was expecting to find

"What are you hiding?" I asked calmly, and Kelly shook her head. I frowned.

"Kelly, what are you hiding?" I asked again,

and she shook her head again. I advanced towards her and changed my tone into a stern one.

"Don't make me ask again, Kelly. What are you hiding?" I asked in a stern voice.

"It's none of your business!" Kelly exclaimed, and I couldn't help the shock that came over my features. Kelly had never been disrespectful to me. This was a first.

"What did you just say?" I asked, narrowing my eyes.

"I said, James, it's none of your business," she repeated, rolling her eyes. I looked at her in shock. She was casually breaking the rules and rolling her eyes at that. Being completely disrespectful to me. I walked to her and picked her up easily. What I saw made me even more disappointed.

"Kelly, what was rule number 3," I asked lowly, looking down at the Nintendo on her bed. I had bought the exact one for her, and it was still at my home, so I didn't understand why she had purchased another one.

"No unnecessary purchases without letting Daddy know," she said in a small voice. Good. She was getting remorseful.

"And what is this?" I asked, looking at her.

"A Nintendo 3DS XL," she mumbled.

"And what did I get you just last week?" I asked patiently, my eyes never leaving her face.

"A Nintendo 3DS XL," she said, and before I could speak, Kelly rushed to justify herself.

"Daddy, I was really bored, and I had forgotten it over at your place. I just wanted to play with something," she explained with tears already in her eyes. Her explanation was meaningful, and I wanted just to let her off the hook. But I knew that I had to punish her because she had broken the rules — two, to be more precise.

"You know I'm going to punish you now, right?" I asked, setting her on the bed and picking up the Nintendo.

"Firstly, you're not going to use this for a while. Then I am going to spank you. You will count out each spank, and at the end, you'll tell me why I punished you and tell me if you think it was justified." I walked towards her and almost caved in when she looked up at me with teary eyes. But I hardened my resolve and put her in my lap after I sat. I bared her bottom and rubbed her ass. I lifted my arm, and I was about to give her the first spank, memories flashed in my mind. I closed my eyes and tried to forget them. I lifted my arm again and placed the first spank on her ass.

"One," Kelly screamed out. I lifted my arm again to give her the second spank, but I found that I was unable to. The flashbacks were deafening.

"Dad, please stop hurting Mom!" a really younger James screamed, holding his father's arm. The latter jerked his arm and sent James flying...

"Promise me you'll never hurt a woman. Promise me. You won't ever make a woman suffer like your father made me suffer. Promise me, James," a frail woman said, holding the hand of her young son.

This one was sobbing as he said, "I promise."

I shook my head suddenly and came back to the present. I saw Kelly there with her bum exposed and me about to hit it. After my promise to my mother. I quickly buttoned her onesie, placed her on the bed, and stood up. I couldn't do it.

"Daddy?" Kelly asked, the confusion in her voice apparent.

"I'll be back," I said and left the house as if I had the devil chasing me.

***

I had called up Kyle, Ryan, and David, the other Daddy Doms I had met at the kink party. We had stayed in touch, and they were incredibly helpful at any time I needed help. So I called them for a drink. I didn't know what to do anymore. And once again, like a coward, I had left Kelly all alone. I knew that aftercare was extremely important. And I could just imagine how she was feeling at home all alone, with the person she called Daddy not even present to comfort her.

"Hey, man," Kyle said. He was staring at me, curiously. I sighed. It hadn't even been a full day since the whole spanking thing, and I was sure I already looked like crap.

"Hey man," I returned his greeting, then picked up my glass of whiskey again and shook it in the glass. Just at the moment, David and Ryan entered. They both frowned when they spotted me.

"What's wrong, man?" It was David, and I sighed.

"It's that obvious, isn't it?" I said tiredly.

"You look like shit," this time around, it was Ryan. I sighed and buried my hand in my hair, then raked it through. I was a mess. They stared at me for a while, presumably waiting for me to tell them why I had called them here. I started hesitantly.

"Have you, have you ever had a hard time spanking your little?" I asked. I fully expected them to burst into laughter, but all they did was stare at me with worry.

"What happened?" David asked. I explained what had happened, and Ryan let out a whistle.

"So your past won't let you discipline her?" he asked, and I nodded miserably.

"I want to be the best Daddy I can be to Kelly. And I know punishing her when she does wrong is one of the steps. But how do I do that when I keep being such a fucking headcase." I said, looking miserable.

"Hey man, take it easy. It mustn't be easy on you either. And you stressing about it isn't going to make it any better. Maybe you should talk to Kelly. She's a sweet girl. She'll understand," Kyle said. The others nodded in agreement and I looked at them before sighing.

"Thank you for your help," I replied. Speaking with the guys had genuinely made me feel better. It had made me feel good, telling them my problem, but I doubted I was going to follow that piece of advice. I didn't want Kelly to see that fucked up part of me yet. I knew it was unfair since she had already confided in me. But I guess I just wasn't ready.

"Thanks, guys," I said as we all made to leave. We had spent a little more time with each other, and I couldn't say I regretted it. I got into my car and drove towards Kelly's house.

I removed the key she had given me and used it to open the door. It was already dark, so I knew she was probably asleep since it was already weekend. I walked to the bedroom quietly. I undressed and walked to the bed softly. I put on the night lamp for a bit, and my heart broke when I saw the tear tracks on her cheeks. I turned it off because I couldn't bear the sight any longer. I slid into the bed and gathered her into my arms.

"I'm sorry, princess. I love you," I whispered and kissed her forehead and smoothed her hair. I silently swore to myself that it was the last time I was going to try to spank her. I was going to be better than her no-good former Daddy.

"Daddy? Is that you?" She called out sleepily.

"Yes, it's me. Sleep now, baby," I said. I held her like that until I fell asleep.

Chapter 5

Kelly's POV

For some time, it was like James had been avoiding me. I knew he had work. I had work too. I knew he was busy. But every time I called him, he made up some excuse. I felt so hurt. I didn't know what I had done wrong. And I really wanted to know so I could work on it. Or was it that he had gotten tired of me and couldn't bear to be my Daddy any longer? Because I was honestly quite tired of waiting like this with no contact at all with him. I mean yes, I had Thea and my other friends from the kink parties. But it just wasn't the same. There were some things I could talk to James about that I couldn't tell anyone else. And there were lots of things I was itching to tell him. But he wasn't available. And that made me sad, so I made up a plan. I was going to pay him a surprise visit at the hospital. He would have no choice but to talk to me and tell me exactly what I had done wrong. I went to his hospital after my shift and walked to the lobby. The hospital was big. But I had been there before, so I knew my way through it. I walked to the pediatric section, which I knew was where James was.

There was an older woman standing behind a desk. I walked to her and asked, "Hi. Is Dr. James Saunders still on duty?" I was polite, so I fully expected her to answer the question. I wasn't prepared for the nasty look she gave me before asking, "And who would you be?" I had changed out of my scrubs, so I looked down at my body to see if there was anything amiss. But I couldn't find anything to warrant her mean look.

"I'm his fiancé," I said, obviously lying. But I knew if I said anything else, she wouldn't give me the time of day and I really needed this to work.

"Well, if you were his fiancé, you'd know if

he were or duty or not, wouldn't you?" the woman asked with a smug smile on her face. I sighed and stared at her.

"I don't know his schedule. And he's a doctor. It changes. So even if I did know what his schedule looks like, I can't guarantee I'm right."

"Look ma'am–" she started but was interrupted by James.

"What's going on here?" he asked in his deep voice staring at both of us. I was tempted to run towards him and hug him, but at this point, I wasn't even sure about the reception he would give me. And I didn't want to be embarrassed in front of the rude receptionist.

James crooked his finger at me with a puzzled look on his face, and I went towards him. I hugged him and took in his scent.

"Oh, Doctor James, I apologize. I thought she was just lying when she said she was your fiancé," the receptionist said with a sheepish look on her face. I fought the urge to stick my tongue out at her. I was getting mature.

"It's okay. Next time you answer her questions," he said and muttered a small "let's go" to me. We walked out, and he led me to the parking lot. It was all very silent, and I honestly didn't know what to say at this point. I mean, I had burning questions on my mind. But I didn't want to ridicule myself. I wasn't going to force myself on someone who didn't want me.

"Fiancé, huh," he said as he started the car and started driving towards his house.

"I didn't want our hidden relationship to be exposed, but you gave me no choice," I said with a nonchalant shrug. I didn't even look at him.

"Hidden relationship? That's how you feel?" James asked, and I shrugged my shoulders again. Maybe coming here was a bad idea. But I just wanted to see my Daddy.

"Look at me when I'm talking to you," he said, and I pretended not to hear him. My head was turned towards the window, and I was looking blankly out of the window.

"Kelly," he called.

"Yeah," I answered after a short while. I aimed to provoke him. I was going to break all the rules in such a way that he would have no choice but to become my true Daddy and give me a punishment. I looked at him through the corner of my eye and saw that his fists were clenched tight on the steering wheel. Good. He was getting mad. I decided to up everything a little.

"Daddy?" I said.

"Yes, Kelly," he said, and it was so obvious that he was pissed. First of all, he never called me Kelly. And secondly, he was clenching his teeth so hard that I was scared they were going to break.

"I. You said to tell you when I broke a rule, right?" I asked as innocently as I could.

"Yes, I did. What did you do?" James asked, and I could tell that he had managed to get some of his anger under control. The devil side of me wanted to spark it up again and make it even worse.

"I... yesterday, I touched myself, Daddy. It

was so fucking good. And besides, there was no one else to do it for me," I said with a sad sigh.

"Where did you touch yourself?" he asked, and I smiled to myself. I like that he actually cared.

"At the hospital, Daddy," I said, pretending to misunderstand him.

"You touched yourself at the hospital?" He asked, and I almost dropped the act and told him that I had been a good girl.

"Yes, Daddy. I did. I'm sure everyone could smell how wet my pussy was." I replied. I was going to break all those rules today. He should just watch and see. James stopped the car and stared at me for a while. Without saying anything, he started the car again and practically flew us to his house. My heart was beating so fast, and I let out a sigh of relief when we reached, and he parked in the garage. As soon as I got out of the car, he came to me and took my hand, dragging me into the house.

"Let me go!" I exclaimed, dragging my feet on the floor. James didn't even pretend he was listening to me. Just continued dragging me. I dug in my steps and refused to move anymore. And that was when he picked me up like a sack of potatoes and put me over his shoulders. I started screaming and kicking, shouting out obscenities. He walked to the bedroom and dumped me on the bed. I sat up and looked at him. He didn't do anything to me, just started walking up and down in the room. I was incredulous. I have provoked him so badly, and all he was going to do was make a hundred steps around the room? I was frustrated at this point. I didn't know what to do next, so I picked up my sippy cup from where it usually stood and threw it at him. He stopped and stared at me with surprise on his face. I took a stuffie this time around and aimed right for his stupid perfect face.

"Kelly stop," James said, but I paid him no mind. I kept throwing things at him. I wanted a reaction. I wanted it now.

"I hate you," I said lowly, then I started screaming it. "I hate you, I hate you, I hate you, I hate-" I was cut off by James kissing me.

"You hate me, huh?" he said, and I swallowed.

Was he going to punish me now? I thought a slight panic flowed through my body making my eyes go wide. What he did next shocked me. He took hold of my shirt and tore it. I looked at him with wide eyes. I was wearing a short rayon skirt, and he couldn't tear that, so he just dragged it down a little roughly. He tore my bra and my panties as well, then spread my legs in a jerky movement.

"You hate me, huh?" he asked again in a tone I couldn't place. He had never been this way with me, and I was surprised and turned on at the same time.

"I hate you," I whispered, not even sure of what I was saying anymore. He knelt in front of the bed, and his tongue brushed my clit. I almost screamed, but I held it in.

"You hate it when I do this?" he asked, then before I could answer, his tongue went back to my clit. This time it did more than kiss it. He laved hungrily at it, and I couldn't help but moan out. Then his fingers found my already wet and pulsating hole. He started off right away with two fingers, and I screamed when he started thrusting them into my wet heat. He lifted his head from my clit.

"You like that you little slut, you like me fingering your pussy, huh? Look how wet and messy you are. I can feel your hole clenching around my fingers," he said. I couldn't even say a word. I just kept on moaning and clutching at his head. He bent again and removed his finger, sending his tongue directly into my hole. He thrust it in and out of me like it was a little erection. I was writhing on the bed. I placed both my hands on his head and started lifting my lips to meet his tongue.

"Yes, Daddy. Please, Daddy," I screamed, riding his tongue. I screamed as my orgasm came over me. When I came down from my high, I was panting loudly, and my legs were still shaking. I watched James stand up and approach me. He held my face in his hand and looked at me, then kissed me. I responded immediately. There was no fight for dominance because we already knew who had won. When the kiss ended, he said, "Do you still hate me?" I looked away.

How could I even hate him? I thought as I rolled my eyes and kissed him again.

Chapter 6

"Can we talk now? You don't hate me anymore?" James asked, and I sighed. We were in bed, and he was behind me, we were spooning. I wasn't wearing a thing, and neither was he. I could feel his erection on my ass, but I wasn't going to let it distract me. We had to have a serious conversation.

"I don't hate you, James. I'm sorry about my behavior. I'm just baffled. I thought you wanted this. I don't want you to feel as if I'm forcing you to be my Daddy," I confessed, holding on to the arm that was on my boobs. James was silent for some time, and I sighed a little. I wanted this to work out. I didn't want to come off as that little that was too pushy or anything. I had already been in a bad relationship before. I didn't want another one. Because I didn't think I would be able to survive the heartbreak.

"I want this, Princess. I want it as much as you do, maybe more. I need you. I need you needing me. I need you wanting me. I never want it to end. But I just have so many things on my mind," he explained, and I frowned.

"Things on your mind?" I turned with difficulty so our eyes could meet. I found it better to communicate when I could see the emotions that were crossing his face.

"My past. My past keeps me from doing all this with you," Daddy said. He sounded so sad that I felt my heart break a little. I put my small hand on his face and smoothed it.

"Daddy, you can talk to me. I'm your little. We have to trust each other, remember?" I reminded him then placed a kiss on his cheek.

"I know this baby girl," was all he said. I waited and looked at him. His eyes were closed, and his Adam's apple moved as he swallowed. I didn't want to push him. I wanted to give him the same respect he had given me. I loved him. But it was hard because seeing him like this was killing me. I wanted to do something to make him feel better. And I knew that him talking about whatever was bothering him would be a good start.

"My father hit my mother," Daddy started. I looked up at him with surprise in my eyes. His eyes were still closed. It was almost like he didn't want me to *see* him if that made sense.

"He started after her first miscarriage. I was seven at the time. I was way too young, even to understand what a miscarriage was. And too young to defend the woman who had put me in this world." I took James's hands into mine and kissed them. My heart reached out to him, and I felt so sad that he had to experience something like that at such a young age.

"He apologized and all that. Said he'd never do it again. It was frustration, he said. But I saw my mother wither. She was never the same. Then he hit her again. I was ten this time. I was older. But what could a ten-year-old boy do against a robust man in his forties?

"He would do it repeatedly until it became a routine. My mother was late for work. He hit her. My mother made his food late. He hit her. His food was cold. He hit her. He found every excuse to hit her," James said as his lip was sneered in disgust, and I wanted just to hold him forever. I felt so sad that I couldn't do anything just to make him better instantly, even though I knew that things didn't work like that.

"Then my mother announced she was pregnant. I was twelve by this time. Things got better. He stopped hitting my mother. He treated her like an egg. She wasn't to do anything at home. And if she did, he scolded her. He urged her to quit her job, pretending that the stress was going to be too much for her to bear. And for a while, it actually seemed like things were looking up.

"Then my mother lost the baby. Everything went downhill from there. He came back home from the hospital in a rage. He locked me up in my closet. I didn't know how much time I spent there.

I was let out sometime after by a neighbor. She drove me to the hospital. The looks she kept on giving me were telltale of something bad happening.

"Without even asking, I knew it was my mother. When I got to the hospital, she was laying there in bed. She looked like a shell. She looked very weak. And tired. But she smiled at me. And told me to come to her. I started crying. I didn't even know how I knew it. But I knew she wasn't going to make the night.

"She asked me one thing only. She asked me to promise never to hit a woman. I remember her exact words. They will never leave my mind. That night when I was supposed to punish you, I couldn't. I kept on thinking about her. And I kept on thinking of what she would say if she witnessed me in a position like that," James explained. He was silent after that. He opened his eyes, and I could see the tears glistening. I reached out impulsively and kissed his chin.

"Daddy," I said, then I hugged him. I knew

he wasn't going to cry. But seeing him so emotionally weak killed me.

"Daddy, I'm sorry that happened to you. And I love you even more after hearing this. But Daddy, you said you needed me to need you, right? I need you to do this. I need you to punish me. When I do wrong, you correct me. It makes me feel loved. I feel loved when you correct me for my wrongdoings. Think of it that way. I'll understand if you still don't want to." I didn't even know if I had made sense at all. But Daddy kissed me then hugged me even tighter to him. That was how we fell asleep, hugging to each other.

***

I woke up the next morning. Then I panicked. It was Thursday. I was supposed to be at work. I looked at the bedside clock and saw that it was almost ten in the morning. In a panic, I jumped out from the bed and ran to the bathroom. After brushing my teeth, I took a quick shower then I stopped. What was I going to wear? James had torn my clothes yesterday. And it would be so strange for me to walk in with men's clothes. Or with a onesie. I didn't think I could bear the eyes of everyone of me when I got out of the car. I tied a towel around my body and went in the search for James. I found him in the kitchen, making breakfast.

"Daddy? Why didn't you wake me up? I'm late for work, and I have nothing to wear," I complained, walking towards him.

"Baby, don't worry about that. You're not going into work today. Or tomorrow. I called in sick for you," he said, and I widened my eyes. Was this man, okay?

"Why?" I asked, confused.

"We're going on a vacation. We're going to Hawaii," he exclaimed with a smile. I squealed. "For real Daddy?" I exclaimed.

"Yes, Princess. For real," he said, and I jumped up into his arms. My towel slipped. I widened my eyes then looked at him through my lashes.

"Don't give me that look, Missy. If you don't want me to bend you over and slide right into your wetness, you'd better go the bedroom and wait for me to dress you.

"Yes, Daddy," I said coyly and giggled as he slapped my ass as I ran to the room. I sat dutifully and waited for him, playing with my stuffies. I looked up when he got into the room, and I smiled happily.

"Daddy!" I exclaimed then lifted my arms.

"Princess," Daddy said with a smile, and I giggled. He lifted me and put me on his lap. He kissed me then placed me on the bed. I watched as he went to the drawers and pulled out a onesie, sockies, and a diaper. Then he came and popped my paci into my mouth, and I started sucking on it. After he changed me successfully, he carried me to the dining table. There was a high chair for me already, so he made me sit there and put food in front of me. He removed the pacifier from my mouth and placed it on a clean tissue. Then he tied a bib around my neck. I loved Daddy feeding me, so I gave him the puppy eyes until he sat and started feeding me.

"Good girl. You aren't too messy," he said when he was done feeding me. I preened at the praise and smiled up at him. He went ahead and put me on a mat in the living room with my toys, a blankie, and my sippy cup on it. I started playing, but then I got bored and held my blankie to me. I wanted to sleep. I must have actually fallen asleep because the next thing I knew, Daddy was waking me up to come to the car.

"Daddy? Where are we going?" I asked, rubbing at my eyes.

"Stop rubbing your eyes. You're going to hurt them. And we are going to the airport," he responded. I let him carry me, and I snuggled into his arms. He put me in the car and put my seatbelt on with a pillow under my head. I fell asleep again. I had no recollection of how everything happened, but the next thing I knew, I was on a bed, and Daddy was sleeping behind me. I frowned. Had we already reached? I hadn't slept that long.

"Daddy," I whispered. I shook him a little and watched as his nose twitched when he woke up.

"Yes, Princess," he answered groggily.

"Where are we?" I asked in a hushed voice.

"On the plane, baby girl," he answered, and I frowned. I thought we were going to take a commercial flight? I asked him.

"No, baby. A friend of mine gave me this as a loan," Daddy explained then said, "Go to sleep Princess." My mouth was still wide open, but I forced myself to lay next to Daddy. Thea was still bugging me about the $150 I had borrowed from her when we were in nursing school. And my Daddy's friends gave him planes to borrow. Wow. It must be nice to be that rich.

***

We reached sometime after and I was so excited. We were in a very beautiful house that had its own private beach, and I just couldn't wait to explore everything. Daddy had packed up everything, including bikinis. He had bought them, though, because they still had tags on, so we changed and headed down to the beach. I was running up and down, and I ignored Daddy when he told me to slow down. I kept on running all over the place. And every time I saw a shell, I stopped to pick it up.

"Slow down, Princess," I heard again, but I pretended not to hear. All of a sudden, a wave crashed into me, and the force of it almost pulled me in. When it finally receded, I saw another wave. But this time, it was in the form of a human. Daddy had a thunderous look on his face as he walked towards me.

"Come. We'll see whether you will disobey again after this," Daddy said, and I widened my eyes. Did this mean he was going to punish me? I swallowed. Instead of being scared, I was kinda excited. We walked to the house in silence, and I could feel the anger coming off Daddy in waves.

We reached the bedroom, and he said, "Remove your bottoms." I obeyed and waited for the next command.

"Come. Lay in my lap," Daddy said, sitting on the bed. I walked to him and did as he said.

"Now I'm going to give you twenty spanks. Ten for putting your life in danger. And then for not listening to me, you'll get another ten. You count out each. If you don't, we'll start all over." James had a slight grin on his face, and it made me wonder if he was actually feeling better about spanking me or if he was just pretending. I swallowed and closed my eyes, waiting for the impact. It didn't come when I expected it to. But I flinched in pain. Daddy had to spank me again to remind me to start counting. By the time we reached ten, the tears were already rolling down my eyes. I didn't want to cry out loud tho. I didn't want Daddy to think I was hurting and stop the punishment. When we reached twenty, Daddy immediately pulled me up, and his expression got sad when he saw my tears.

"Are you okay?" he asked, sounding concerned. I loved it that he always checked to make sure that everything was still fine. I smiled and kissed his thigh.

"Yes, Daddy. Thank you for punishing me," I said. He stood up with me in his arms and walked to the bathroom. He ran a bath and undressed me totally. When the bath was ready, he put me in it and washed me thoroughly, making sure to remind me that he loved me and that he was punishing me for my own good.

"I love you, Daddy," I said when he kissed my shoulder for like the hundredth time.

"I love you too, Princess. Don't ever forget," he said, and I misted up a little. Then he got into the bath with me. We stayed there until the water got cold. Then we got out. Then we went to the bedroom and cuddled in bed. I closed my eyes and just enjoyed the feel of his body against mine without anything sexual attached to it.

Chapter 7

After the weekend, I hadn't heard from Daddy. He had dropped me off at my place, kissed me hard, and passionately then told me to be "a good girl." I was so confused because his words sounded final and loving at the same time. I didn't know what to make of it. But now, here we were, a day later, and I hadn't heard from him. This was getting annoying. We were fine one day and then the next, he just ghosted me. It wasn't a very nice feeling. I was lonely. Yes I had friends. But Thea wasn't into the lifestyle so she wouldn't understand. And my other friends who were actually littles would just tell me to be patient. Their daddies were always there, so they didn't know how it felt to be lonely like this. Maybe I was being dramatic because it was just a day. But I needed attention. And Daddy was the only person who knew how to give me the kind of attention I wanted.

When I got back home from work, I received a call from him, and it put me right into a good mood. He told me he was busy and that he was going to make the effort of coming over the next day. I was sad he wasn't going to come at that instant. But I felt relieved that he didn't want to leave me. These abandonment issues weren't things you got rid of in one day. I got another call. From an unknown number. I frowned. But I picked it up. It could be important.

"Hello?" I said hesitantly, hoping it wasn't Alex or something.

"Kelly?" The person said. The voice sounded vaguely familiar, but I couldn't place it.

"Yes. This is Kelly. Who's speaking, please?" I asked, hoping the person didn't get offended and hang up or something. Trust me. It had happened to many times to count to me.

"It's Olivia," was the reply. I frowned, then my eyes widened in realization. I had met Olivia when I had just gotten with Alex. We had gotten along very well, and we told each other everything. But she had to move with her Daddy, and that was when we stopped communicating with each other.

"Oh my God, it's been like five years," I exclaimed.

"Not that long. But yeah," she said, laughing.

"How have you been?" Olivia asked, and I smiled.

"I've been good babes. And you?" I asked.

"Not too good," she replied.

"Oh, why," I asked, worried. I mean, we hadn't spoken to each other in years. But she was still my friend and friendship didn't die off, even if communication died off.

"I.. can we meet up and talk? Like right now?" Olivia asked, and the sadness in her voice made my heart break a little. I loved Olivia still, and seeing her sad was not something I appreciated.

"Yes, babes. Let's meet up, of course. You're in Florida, right? Meet me at the Chinese restaurant next to Weiss Memorial," I said, and we hung up. I got dressed again, and I rushed to get to her. Olivia had always had my back when we were still in contact. And I wanted to be there for her as well. When I reached the restaurant, she was already there. I spotted her sitting with some luggage next to the table. I frowned. Her eyes looked puffy, and her hair was messed up. And this was Olivia we were talking about. Olivia was one of the most glamorous persons I knew. Her hair was always done, her nails and makeup as well. So to see her looking so haggard, meant something was actually wrong. I walked to her briskly and sat at her table.

"Babes?" I said. She lifted her head and broke into a smile. She was still very beautiful, that was for sure.

"Kelly. You came," Olivia said, and I smiled.

"Of course, I came Oli. You said you needed my help," I replied.

"I don't know... I thought since we hadn't spoken to each other in so long, you would actually come. Thank you Kels," she said, and I nodded.

"Have you ordered anything? Or maybe you should come home instead and get a to-go box?" I suggested, and she nodded gratefully. After we had gotten our food which wasn't long after because the restaurant was virtually empty, we went to my car. We put in the luggage, and I started the car.

"So I'm not going to ask you any questions now because you look really tired. But when we reach, you will take a shower– because you look like shit–, eat, rest, and then we'll talk," I said. Olivia laughed a little. It was an encouraging sound, and I felt happy that I had caused it.

"Deal," she said. The ride home was silent. I knew she was thinking hard because every time I stole a look at her, she had a sad, faraway look on her face. I wanted to hug her.

We reached home, and I showed her where to keep everything. We sat in the living room and started eating. I wanted to ask her about her Daddy, but I had a feeling that everything that was happening right now was because of him. So I kept my mouth shut and just watched her. I guess she was going to talk when she was ready.

"How have you been, Kels?" Olivia asked, and I sighed of happiness.

"And Alex? How is he? Where is he actually?" She asked. I had never told her what he had really been doing to me or how we really was behind closed doors. It wasn't that I didn't feel I could trust her, it was that I wasn't sure how to tell her all the things he had been doing to me without sounding pathetic and even more humiliated. I tensed up at that name. It brought up too many bad memories. And it reminded me of too many things. I cleared my throat.

"Well, Alex is no longer my Daddy," I said, looking away.

"What happened?" she asked with a sympathetic tilt to her head. I sighed.

"A lot of things. But it all comes to the fact that he was abusive, and he cheated on me. Multiple times and in front of me," I explained. I hated going into detail, but I felt she had to know, I guess. Her Daddy and Alex used to be friends.

"Your Daddy didn't tell you all this?" I asked.

"Please don't call him my Daddy. His name is Mike," she said with an angry look on her face. I frowned. So I was right. Mike had indeed caused her a world of pain.

"Oh, sorry. What happened?" I asked.

"If you don't want to talk about it, it's okay." I didn't want her to force herself to do something that she was later on going to regret. I wanted her to be ready when she told me anything.

"No, don't worry about it. It's actually because of that that I am here right now," she said, and I frowned. But I didn't interrupt.

"Mike and I were happy. You know we moved to California and all that. I honestly thought we would be together for a long while. I was thinking long term. Maybe even marriage," she explained, and I nodded. I knew just how committed those two were to each other.

"We saved up. Made a down payment on the house. But sweetie, what he didn't tell me was he made it in his name only. And every time I asked him, he told me not to worry about it. That it was Daddy stuff." I frowned. That was exactly what Alex used to tell me as well, and we all know how that ended.

"Then a few days ago, he tells me he's getting married," Olivia continued. My mouth dropped.

"What?" I exclaimed.

"Yes. He said he was getting married. And that this lifestyle was just experimentation. That's what he told me. He said he wasn't ready to take care of someone his whole life. He basically said a bunch of stuff that I'm not even ready to repeat yet," she said and laughed sadly. I wanted to hold her, but I refrained myself. I knew from experience that it was just best to let her finish first. Besides, I didn't want her to start crying before she even got to finish the story.

"Kelly, I honestly don't know how I

survived that. I didn't even cry in front of him. I don't know how I did it, but I didn't break down, not even once. I stood there, stonily and listened to all his bullshit." I felt so proud of her. Crying in front of people who didn't even care about you was just letting them in on your weaknesses. It never ever worked in your favor. It was just you showing them how desperate you are.

"Then I talked about the house. And I basically asked him what we were going to do about it. Guess what Kels? He had never even put my name on the title. So all my savings, all my efforts were for nothing. He just used me, Kels. He used me, and I hate him for that." That was when the dam burst. Olivia started sobbing. I moved towards her and took her into my arms. I didn't even know what to say. Losing the person you thought loved you then losing all your savings as well. Damn. I didn't even want to imagine how she felt in that moment.

"I couldn't stay there anymore, Kelly. I couldn't stay in that godforsaken town. Then I'd have to look at his face every day, he and his stupid beautiful wife, entering the house that I used my savings to pay for. I just couldn't. I had nowhere else to go. No other friend. I'm sorry for just barging into your life," Olivia said as she started to cry.

"Hey, babes. It's okay. Don't cry. I'm here for you. You're my friend, and I love you. You can count on me any time. Okay?" I said, and she nodded. We just sat there for some time, me hugging her until her tears subsided.

"Thank you so much, Kels. It means a lot." As I was looking at her sad face, the best idea I think I had ever had came into my head.

"Wait. Why don't you just move in with me? We understand each other better than most people do. And we get along well. So as you're getting on your feet, move in with me?"

"Do you really mean this?" Olivia asked. The surprise was evident on her face.

"Yes, babes. Move-in. I love you. And I want to support you in any way I can," I said, and she started sobbing again

"Thank you so much, Kelly. You are such an amazing friend. I don't know what I would have done without you," Olivia said.

***

About thirty minutes later, we had called Thea over because she had complained about not spending enough time with me, and the "squad" was complete. Even though Thea didn't participate in the lifestyle, she was still cool with us talking about it around her.

"So tell us about your Daddy," Olivia said. We were sitting in the bedroom, watching a movie. Even though I'm pretty sure none of us had a clue on what it was about.

"My Daddy is the best in world. I honestly love him so much. Okay, you might feel that I'm too hasty. But he's so good to me. He makes a conscious effort to be what I need, and he tries his best to give me what I need. I really love him," I said dreamily. Both of them were quiet. I looked at them and raised my brows.

"What?" I asked, looking from Olivia to Thea and back to Olivia.

"It's just. I've never see you this way. Not even with Alex," Thea said, looking hesitantly at Olivia, who nodded. I blushed.

"Maybe I feel more? I don't know. But James is good to me," I stated with a bright smile.

"We're happy for you, babes. And I hope this lasts. If he hurts you, I don't care if he's 7ft15. I'll hunt him down and rip his balls." This was said by Thea, who was the shortest human being on Earth at 5'1. As we rolled around the floor laughing, I felt a glow of happiness in my heart that I had not felt in years. Then Olivia spoke up.

"I'm happy for you love. You deserve this happiness and more. You are a wonderful person," Olivia said. I wiped the tear that was threatening to fall, and I dragged both of them into a group hug. I couldn't ask for better friends.

Chapter 8

James was supposed to come today. I knew that I wasn't supposed to take any major decisions without him. But last night, when Olivia had cried in front of me, I honestly felt like I had no other choice. She was my friend, and I wanted to support her in every way.

"So have you thought about what you're going to tell your Daddy?" she asked, and I sighed, then shook my head.

"I don't know. I'll just explain what happened to him and he'll understand. He's a great Daddy," I said and smiled.

"He sure does sound like one," Olivia said, and I couldn't help but notice that her tone sounded wistful.

"Don't worry, babes. You'll find a Daddy who will love you the way you're supposed to be love. And he'll see to all your needs," I said, emphasizing the word all. I hugged her, and she leaned into me.

"I'll go the bedroom for a bit," she said, then she walked to the room. I watched her walk away and sighed. Olivia was such a beautiful person. She deserved way more than all she was getting. At that moment, Daddy came in. My eyes widened.

"Daddy! You're here early," I exclaimed, standing from the couch and going into his arms.

"Yes Princess. You didn't want me to come?" Daddy teased, and I laughed.

"Of course, I did. I missed you so much yesterday. I thought you were ignoring me," I confessed, putting my head down. He carried me to the couch and sat me in his lap

"And how could I ever ignore you? You're my princess. I always try my best to make time for you," he said and placed a kiss on my lips. "So what did you do yesterday? And what's that?" he asked, looking at the ashtray. I widened my eyes. I had forgotten entirely that Olivia smoked. And she had left her ashtray in the living room. I was going to kill that girl.

"I.. uh, it's mine?" I said or more like asked.

"I know you don't smoke. What are you hiding from me, Kelly?" Daddy asked, and I bit my lip.

"Nothing, Daddy," I said, pushing him onto the couch.

"Are you lying to me right now?" Daddy asked with narrowed eyes and a tone that said I'd better tell him the truth. I sighed and nodded.

"What was rule number 4?" James asked, looking at me with a smirk.

"Never lie to Daddy," I said with a pout. I hated that I couldn't get away with anything.

"And what did you just do?" James questioned, reaching out and tucking my hair behind my ears.

"I lied Daddy," I said, looking down at my feet.

"Now you'll tell me what exactly you lied to me about. Starting from whose ashtray that is,"

James demanded. When Daddy got like this, I knew not to mess with him, so I hurried to tell him what had happened.

"Well, Daddy, I have a friend over. She came in yesterday. And she didn't have anywhere else to go. So I told her to move in. Wait! Daddy! Before you say anything, I know I should have told you about it. But she's really stranded, and her Daddy left her. I just felt so sad," I trailed out and lay my head on his shoulder.

"Go get your friend," Daddy ordered as he pushed me gently off his lap. I walked to the room and saw Olivia sitting on the bed. I knew from the expression her face that she had been listening to everything

"I hope I didn't get you into trouble?" she asked with a worried expression on her face.

"No, don't worry about it. He'll probably punish me, and that'll be all about it," I explained and held her hand. We walked to the living room, and Daddy was standing with his back to us.

"Daddy," I called, and he turned.

"Hi," Olivia said, waving. I could tell that Daddy was impressed by Olivia's features. We were the same height, but our appearances were very different. Olivia was a blonde with startlingly clear green eyes. She had the most beautiful features that beckoned you to her. I hadn't met someone yet that wasn't impressed with her. She was a very beautiful woman.

"And who might you be?" Daddy asked as he approached us.

"I'm Olivia. Kelly's friend. Please don't punish her! She didn't do anything. She was just being a good friend to me," Olivia said, and I held my breath waiting for Daddy's reaction

"So she told you I was going to punish her, huh?" Olivia didn't answer, just bit her lip. I sighed. He was probably going to up the punishment now.

"What we are going to do is, I'll give Kelly's punishment, and you, Olivia, will watch. Is that clear?" Daddy asked, and I let out a sigh of relief. I knew he would never push my limits, but sometimes I got inexplicably scared. I nodded, and

Olivia took that as her cue to nod as well.

"Come to the bedroom now," he said, and we followed him dutifully. Daddy sat at the edge of the bed, motioned for Olivia to sit opposite him. He gave me a look, and I already knew what it meant. I climbed into his lap and took in a deep breath as he removed my clothes. I wasn't scared he was going to hurt me. I was just nervous because it was the first time that I was getting punished in front of someone else. I swallowed as he repeated what he always did.

"Count out after each spank. If not, I'll start all over again. I'll give you ten spanks," he said, and I nodded, even though he didn't technically needed me to agree. The first spank was a surprise. But for some reason, my pussy clenched on nothing, already getting moist.

"One," I shouted. The next one was even more arousing.

"You're getting wet. You like that, huh?" Daddy said, then he placed a light spank on my pussy. I gasped spread my legs even more. After five spanks, I turned to look at Olivia, and I almost smiled. She had that look on her face. I knew she was turned on. I had seen her turned on before when we had had scenes at the kink club. And with the way she kept on changing her positions in the chair. Our eyes met, and I winked at her. She blushed.

"Look how wet your pussy is," Daddy said when he was done spanking me.

"Do you want me to touch you? To finger you until you come?" James teased.

"Yes, please, Daddy," I whined, gyrating my ass in his lap. He slapped my ass lightly then he asked a question that made me pause a little.

"Do you think I should let her cum Olivia?" James asked.

"Um, yes, sir," Olivia replied. I could tell from Olivia's voice that she was just as shocked. Daddy slapped my ass again, then traced the outline of my wetness lightly with his finger. I clenched it and whined a little. Then finally, he inserted the finger to the hilt and fucked it slowly.

"More, please, Daddy," I said. Daddy added another finger, then another, and started thrusting fast. I held his wrist and started riding his fingers, moaning out. At this point, I didn't even care if Olivia was in the room or not. I just wanted to cum.

"Yes, Daddy," I screamed as the orgasm hit me. Then I let go of his hand and slumped in his lap.

***

After a bath, Daddy changed both Olivia and I. We were both wearing onesies, hers was purple, and mine was pink. We were sitting in the living room when he brought out a mat and placed a couple of toys on it. There was something about seeing all my toys in one place that made me regress. I couldn't even explain it. Once I had my pacifier in my mouth, my diaper and onesie on, and my toys placed out, I just couldn't help it. Apparently it was the same for Olivia. Daddy was watching us play with a smile on his face.

"Want to have a team party?" I asked Olivia. My age space was between 8 to 10, but I think Olivia was younger. Because she couldn't even articulate properly.

"Tea Party!" she exclaimed, and I smiled.

"Daddy, can we have a tea party?" I asked Daddy, turning towards him.

"Sure, Princess. Where's your tea set?" he asked, and I pointed with a tilt to my head.

"Even when you regress, you're bossy," Daddy muttered playfully, but I still heard him. I laughed a little. He brought the tea set. I helped Olivia, who was still playing with her stuffies, to sit properly. I put a cup in front of her. Then I looked up at Daddy.

"Daddy, won't you join us?" I asked, giving him my infamous puppy eyes.

"Sure, Princess," he said, then came and sat in one of the chairs. I laughed a little at how ridiculous he looked, but I placed a cup in front of me. I poured the tea into their cups. I laughed when instead of drinking, Olivia took the cup and started hitting it against the table. I looked over at Daddy, who was staring at me already. I blushed, and a feeling of contentment came over me. Then I let out a loud gasp as a great idea came to my head.

"Daddy, why don't you be Olivia's Daddy too?" I asked.

Chapter 9

Today we were heading over to Daddy's house. After the last time, after I had blurted my question, he had scolded me a little. But I knew it was something he wanted as well. So I pushed for it. So when Olivia came out of her regression, I brought it up again. Innocently. Not at all subtly. I just went, "Olivia don't you want my Daddy to be your Daddy as well?" I think she thought I was testing her cause she grew flustered and shook her headfirst. But I knew she was lying. Daddy, too, was lying. They both wanted to be in each other's lives, but they were scared of my reaction. I honestly was okay with it. Olivia was one of my closest friends, and I loved her a lot. And James was my Daddy. I loved him too. And honestly, I didn't mind if we shared this love we had for each other together. Neither of them had agreed, but I was still going to try and convince them because I thought they just needed a little push. So I had convinced Olivia to come with me to Daddy's house.

We reached Daddy's place in record time. When we got in, Daddy was in the living room. He wasn't even surprised to see Olivia with me. He said, "Good. You brought Olivia along," and it left me wondering what exactly he meant by that. But I didn't press and just watched him. He told us both to sit. I looked at Olivia to make sure she was comfortable. I definitely didn't want to drag her into something that she felt weird about. I didn't want to be that friend.

"So I thought about what you said yesterday a lot, Kelly," Daddy started, and I had to curb my victorious smile. I knew that Daddy had been thinking about it. I knew my Daddy.

"And while it is true that Olivia and I don't know much about each other yet, I would love to be her Daddy. Olivia, is this something you would be interested in?" Daddy asked. I felt like squealing. This was the most awesome thing ever. I looked over at Olivia as both Daddy and I waited for a response from her.

"Yes," she said quietly. I knew Daddy didn't like that. He liked it when you speak up loudly and clearly.

"What was that? Speak clearly. And you can call me Daddy if you agree," Daddy added.

"Yes, Daddy," was Olivia's response, and I couldn't help it. I squealed this time around. I jumped from where I was sitting and ran to Daddy and hugged him. Then I placed a kiss on his mouth.

"You're the best Daddy ever, in the whole wide world," I said and kissed him again. He laughed, then held me. Both of us turned out glances towards Olivia, who was still sitting there.

"Come here, little one," Daddy said to Olivia lovingly. Olivia reacted instantly. She ran towards him as well and jumped into his arms. He placed both of us on both his laps.

"Okay, now. I have a surprise for both of y'all. I'll need you to stay patient. I don't want any show of impatience. If not, I'll punish you. Okay?" James instructed, looking more at me than Olivia. I knew I had a way of being impatient, but he didn't need to rub it in.

"Yes, Daddy," we chorused.

"Good," come James's short answer as he set us down on the couch, then went and picked something up from the table. They were blindfolded. He tied both our eyes, starting with Olivia.

"I'll carry both of you to the bedroom. And when I place you on the floor, you're to stay in the same spot. Don't move, okay?" James instructed. I loved it when he did things like this.

"Yes, Daddy," we chorused again. I felt Daddy's arms against my back as he lifted me into his powerful arms. I giggled a little, and Daddy placed a kiss on my forehead. We reached the bedroom, and he set me on a soft and comfortable surface.

"If you peek, I'll know," was all Daddy said before he left the room. I waited for him to come along with Olivia. The urge to just lift the blindfold and peek was extremely strong. But I controlled myself and say dutifully like a good girl. I didn't want to spoil the surprise for all three of us. I heard Daddy's footsteps, and I perked up. After a few rustles, he said, "Okay, now you can lift your blindfolds." I lifted my blindfold slowly, and I was in awe at what I saw. It was an actual nursery. Not just a play spot with a couple of toys. A nursery. I looked at Olivia, and I could tell that she was just as awed as me. The theme of the room was baby pink, which was my favorite color and I think Olivia's as well. There were two cribs in the room and in the cribs were a bunch of stuffies. There was a huge section filled with just toys, and I couldn't wait to play there. Then there was a tea table. There were also video games and a console for us to play.

"I hope you like it." Daddy's voice brought me out of my awestruck state. I looked at him like he was mad.

"Like it? Daddy, we love it. Right, Olivia?" I

asked since she wasn't saying anything. She smiled at me, then turned to Daddy and said, "We do. Thank you, Daddy."

"Thank you, Daddy," I repeated. I stood from wherever Daddy had placed me which was a bean bag by the way and ran to him.

"I love you so much, Daddy. Can we explore?" I asked, clapping my hand.

"Go right ahead, princess. It's your nursery," was Daddy's response. This man really wanted me to love him even more than I did right now. I walked around, touching everything with awe. Alex had never offered me this, not even when we were okay. It was all so new to me, but I loved going around the room and touching everything I could get my hands on.

"When you are done, tell me. We need to go over some things," Daddy said, then left the room.

"Are you sure you really don't mind sharing your Daddy?" Olivia asked as soon as Daddy left the room.

"I wouldn't have proposed if I minded,

right? I love you. I really do. And I want your happiness. I feel that we will be very happy together, all three of us," I explained, and she nodded.

"I love you, Kels," Olivia said, then she pulled me into a long hug.

"Let's go find Daddy," I said, grabbing her hand and running through the house. We smiled at each other then I led her to Daddy's bedroom. I knew he was probably going to be in there. And I was right. He was sitting on the bed, and he looked up when we came in.

"Hi Daddy," I said, and he motioned for us to walk to him. When we reached, he placed each of us on either side of his lap. Then he showed the papers he had been looking at. It was my contract. I felt kind of possessive when I saw it, which was kind of stupid. Why didn't I feel possessive over Daddy? Just over the contract? I sighed and decided not to mull over it more than necessary. It was of no use trying to understand my thoughts sometimes. So I listened to whatever Daddy was saying.

"So I set up more rules. Kelly already knows them. But you don't know them, Olivia. So we'll leave you some time to read. You read them and tell me if you don't understand anything, alright?" James asked, patting my bottom lovingly.

"Yes, Daddy," she replied and started reading. I leaned in Daddy's shoulder and watched her for a while. Then I got bored. I started playing with the collar of Daddy's shirt, and he hugged me close to him.

"Are you sure you're okay with this? I know you're the one who proposed it in the first place, but I want to know that you're completely okay before we proceed to anything," Daddy said, and my heart warmed at his thoughtfulness.
"Yes, Daddy. I love both of you. And I feel we need each other. I don't know why," I explained so he could understand my motives more.

"Olivia's Daddy left her in a really bad state, and she needs love. She's a bit like me, Daddy. She needs you. She needs us," I explained. Daddy looked at me for a while without saying a word. Then he kissed me on the forehead.

"You're a gem. I love you," James said, kissing the top of my head. Soon enough, Olivia was done reading.

"Done?" Daddy asked, and she nodded.

"Is there anything you're not comfortable with?" James asked.

"Uh, yes, Daddy. The smoking rule..." She started, but Daddy interrupted her.

"We will start off slowly, but I want you to drop it. I know you are addicted to it. But for now, we'll go progressively. Okay?" Daddy asked, and Olivia nodded.

"Thank you, Daddy," she said shyly then placed a kiss on his cheek. I was happy.

***

The next day was beautiful. I had never felt that way before. Olivia and I slept with Daddy, and it was honestly one of the best feelings in my life. We were up for the day now and sitting in the dining table, waiting for Daddy to serve us breakfast. Since we were two of us, I doubted that he was going to feed us both. I didn't mind, though. It was going to be tiring if he tried something like that. As he placed the food in front of us, we both said thanks. Then dug in. As soon as Olivia took a bite of her food, though, she said, "Fuck!" I looked up at her then looked at Daddy. He hadn't heard. Because he wasn't looking at us. And he hadn't turned to scold Olivia or anything.

"You need to tell Daddy," I said, looking up at her worriedly. I didn't want to tell on her. But not telling Daddy was going to be breaking two rules. Olivia bit her lip and said, "I know. Let's finish eating." I nodded. At that moment, I started imagining the punishment scene, and I started feeling left out. But I didn't want to be a bad girl either. I didn't want to do something and just to purposely get a spanking from Daddy. So I refrained myself. As Daddy was clearing the plates, Olivia said, "Daddy, I... I broke a rule. I'm sorry,

Daddy. I said a bad word." Her lip was trembling as he looked up at Daddy. He packed up the plates, placed them in the sink, then walked back to us.

"Come. Let's go for your punishment. And baby girl, come along. You're going to watch," he told me, and I stood eagerly. We went to the bedroom.

"I'll give you five spanks, Olivia. Because you told me right away. Come here," Daddy said. Olivia went to him. I watched as he undressed her and put her in his lap. For the first time since I had said Olivia and I should share Daddy, I felt jealous. There was some connection that I couldn't explain in spanking. And seeing Olivia taking advantage of it and not me saddened me. Daddy noticed. "What's wrong, Princess?" he asked, and I sighed a little.

"Can I have a spanking, too, Daddy?" I asked.

"Did you do anything wrong?" Daddy asked, and I shook my head.

"Then why do you want a spanking?" James

asked.

"It makes me feel closer to you," I confessed. Daddy looked at me for a while then beckoned me to him.

"We'll give you three spanks. Count each of them out," he said, then placed me in his lap. I felt fulfilled. Or maybe it wasn't the right word. I just couldn't explain it. Having my Daddy discipline me was something I would always be thankful for and never get tired of.

Chapter 10

It was weekend again, which was the only time Olivia and I could spend time without Daddy. This was because Olivia had found a job. She was working as a secretary at a publishing company. I had my shifts at the hospital, and Daddy did too. Friday, Daddy had picked us up and drove over to his place. We had all missed each other because as soon as Olivia and I saw him, we launched at him with hugs. Hugs he received with just as much affection. I loved just how affectionate Daddy was. He always made sure to give us hugs, kisses, and show us generally that he loved and appreciated us. It wasn't even about sex. I could count the number of times we had had sex. He was just a really awesome Daddy. It was Daddy who woke both of us up the next morning.

"I've run a bath for you. Come to the

bathroom," he said. We had ignored our cribs again and slept with him in his bedroom. In my opinion, it was way better. I loved knowing the fact that my two favorite people were sleeping next to me, and I could reach out and touch them any time. Olivia and I stripped and followed Daddy to the bathroom. I think I squealed a little when I got to the bath. The water was pink! And there were lots of toys floating on it. It was so pretty.

"It's so pretty, Daddy!" Olivia exclaimed, stealing the thoughts right out of my mouth. I nodded, and daddy smiled. I loved it when Daddy smiled.

"You look so handsome when you smile, Daddy," I said, smiling at him. I swear a blush appeared on Daddy's skin! Daddy was blushing!

"Thank you, princess," he said.

"You're all red, Daddy," I teased, and we laughed.

"Get into that bath, little brat," James said, making me giggle. I got into the bath after sticking my tongue at Daddy. Both Olivia and I were in the tub, and I splashed water at her. She laughed, and she retaliated, making both of us giggle.

"Bubbles," Olivia whispered in awe when we splashed the water a little too much and bubbles form. I picked one up and poked at it curiously, then giggle when it bursts. Then I took another and opened my mouth. As I was about to put it on my tongue, Olivia burst it, and we giggled.

"Don't put it anywhere near your mouths," Daddy warned, and we nodded. We kept playing. Then Daddy stopped us. He washed me first, then got me out of the water with instructions to towel myself dry. I used the towel and wiped off all the water I could and watched Daddy as he washed Olivia in the bath. I almost want to go join them again, but Daddy carried Olivia out of the bathtub and ordered her to towel herself dry as well. I watched with fascination as Daddy pulled out the plug, and the water started draining out of the bathtub. And don't ask why I found it fascinating. It just was. We followed Daddy to the room. I sat on the beanbag watching as Daddy changed Olivia.

He put her diaper on, took a cute blue onesie, and made her wear it. Then he put the paci in her mouth. Then it was my turn. It was always so comforting how Daddy took care of me. It was in the little things. How he gave us baths, dressed us, fed us and was just there overall for us. I wanted to be there for him as well. I hoped he was happy.

"Daddy, are you happy with us?" I asked, looking at him intently. I knew Daddy well enough by now to know when he was lying or hurt.

"I am princess. You brighten up my world," Daddy said, then he placed a kiss on my lips. I smiled, satisfied. He wasn't lying. He really was happy with us. And I was happy about that. I wouldn't want to be in a relationship where just one party was happy. It was interesting, hurtful, and draining. When we were both dressed, we went to the part of the nursery that doubled as a playpen. I didn't really want to play, so I watched as Olivia played with her stuffies.

"Is anything wrong, baby?" Daddy asked, and I sighed.

"No, Daddy. I just... my princess parts are tingling," I said in a small voice.

"And you want me to take care of it?" Daddy asked, and I nodded. We went to Daddy's room alongside Olivia. I was excited. This was the first time that I was initiating things, especially now that Olivia was here. And I didn't know how everything was going to go. But I was so excited. As soon as we reached the bedroom, Daddy ordered both of us to take off our clothes. When we did so, he took off our diapers. None of us was wet and messy, so he kissed us and told us we were good girls.

"Both of you, lay in bed," Daddy ordered. We scrambled to obey, and we both did lay, watching him walk around the room. I wanted to know what he was going to tell me to do next.

"Are your princess parts still tingling Kelly?" Daddy asked.

"Yes, Daddy," I responded, hoping that he was going to do something about it.

"What about yours, Olivia?" he continued,

and I risked a glance at Olivia. I didn't know she felt this way too.

"Yes, Daddy," she answers as well.

"Touch yourselves. I want you to spread those pink pussy lips for Daddy, spread them, and touch your hard little clits." I swallowed at the feeling that Daddy's words were giving me, and I followed his instructions. I spread my lower lips and placed a finger on my clit. I rubbed it and let out a low moan, writhing a little when the pleasure increased.

"Now what you're going to do is Olivia, get down. Spread Kelly's lips, and suck on her clit." I watched Olivia as she did what Daddy told her to do. Her soft hands on my lips were such a turn on, and when she took my clit into her mouth, I almost lost it. I closed my eyes and let out a loud moan. This was one of the best feelings in the world.

"Liv..." I moaned out, closing my eyes and threading my fingers through her hair.

"That's enough. Olivia lay back. Kelly do the same thing." It was such a turn on to be hearing

Daddy's orders. I spread Olivia's legs a little, then touched her pussy lightly with my index finger. I opened up her lips and rubbed the clit a little, enjoying how she writhed in pleasure. There was a lot of juice coming from her hole. I bent and took her clit into my mouth, making sure to suck on it.

"Oh yes, Kels. Oh my God, that feels so good," she said, and I preened at the praise.

"That's enough now," Daddy said, and I reluctantly removed my mouth from Olivia's pussy.

"Now, you'll kiss and taste each other." I advanced towards Olivia and placed my hand on her beautiful face. I leaned in for a kiss, and our lips met. Her lips were soft to the touch, and I knew I was going to enjoy this. I deepened the kiss, and I could feel my juices flowing even more as her sweet tongue explored my mouth.

"That's enough," Daddy said, and when we looked at him, he was naked. His hand was stroking his big erection. Then he climbed on the bed as well and lay down.

"Kelly, climb on my cock and ride it. Olivia, come sit on my face," James ordered. I went eagerly. I wanted to shock daddy and please him even more, so before sitting on his cock, I put it in my mouth and sucked on it a little. I knew he liked that by the little groan he released. Then I let go of it with a pop. I straddled his laps and guided his erection into my very wet hole. When he slid to the hilt, I let out a loud moan. I hadn't felt this in so long, and it felt like heaven.

"Don't ride yet," Daddy commanded, and I tried my best to curb my desires. I watched as Olivia straddled Daddy's face, facing me. Then I felt Daddy jerk his hips up, a signal that I could start riding. I placed my hands on both sides of his legs and started riding slowly, enjoying the feeling of his dick against my walls. It was the best feeling in the world. I looked up and saw Olivia, who was also riding his face. I leaned forward and kissed her, enhancing the whole experience even more. Then I let go and let out a huge gasp. It was almost like Daddy had gotten bigger in me. I started riding him even quicker, not minding the sweat that was dripping from my boobs. The pleasure was only intensifying, and I felt like I was going to pass out at any moment from it.

"Oh my God, Daddy," I heard Olivia scream, and I think it sparked my own orgasm. Because at that moment, the waves of pleasure hit me. I kept riding them and screaming, my eyes closed, and my back arched. I continued riding Daddy until he jerked powerfully one last time and put his cum in me. Olivia got down from Daddy's face, and I leaned forward and kissed him. Then kissed her.

"I love you, Daddy. I love you, Olivia," I said as happy tears welled up in my eyes. This was honestly one of the best experiences of my entire life.

Chapter 11

It had been a month since Olivia had come into our lives, and everything was going smoothly. Since all three of us had had sex, it had become a regular thing. Sometimes, Daddy would tell us to each other out. Or one of us would eat the other out while the latter sucked on his cock. It was different from all the experiences I had had before, and I wasn't complaining. Matter of fact, it was something I really enjoyed. After the initial possessiveness, I had felt every time Daddy had to punish Olivia, which wasn't often cause she was a really good girl, everything else had gone really smoothly. It was funny how Alex used to bring littles in front of me to taunt me, and I got jealous. But here I was, sharing a Daddy with one of my closest friends and feeling good about the whole thing. It wasn't that I loved Daddy less. It definitely wasn't the case. Or that I considered Olivia inferior to me or something. That was not it either. I loved my Daddy very much. And I believed without being biased that Olivia was one of the most beautiful people that graced the earth. The thing is I knew and trusted both of them. And maybe my trust was going to backfire, but I didn't think so. I believed all three of us loved each other. And if I was being honest, I had started loving Olivia, more than just a friend. I had just gotten back from work. I got into the house and frowned a little. The house was messy. And with two people like Olivia and I living in it, this house was never messy. We were extremely neat and made sure to keep everything where it was supposed to be, so I didn't understand. Nevertheless, I walked to the bedroom, and I saw that it was even messier than the living room. I frowned.

"Olivia?" I called, wondering where she was.

"In here!" The voice was coming from the bathroom, so I walked there and opened the door.

This room was no exception. It was almost like a hurricane had come and swept through the room, leaving only one side of the stuff on my side untouched.

"What's happening? Why is everything so messy?" I asked, watching her weigh two bottles before throwing them both into a bag.

"And what are you packing?" I questioned, biting my bottom lip.

"I'm so sorry, Kels. I meant to be gone before you came. But I guess since you're here, oh well."

"Where are you moving to?" I asked, a strange feeling coming over me. I didn't like where this was going. And I honestly wasn't sure that I was going to like her answer.

"James didn't tell you? I'm moving in with him," Olivia announced brightly, and I tilted my head to the side. I probably had misunderstood because Olivia didn't just say that she was moving in with my Daddy.

"What did you say? You're moving in with

who?" I asked again. I wasn't the type of get into flights. But I would honestly fight her if she thought she was going to do me dirty like this. Then I was going to meet that bullhead of James and punch him in the face, no matter how hard it hurt my hand.

"I said, I'm moving in with James, and I... The both of us, we reached the conclusion that I will be his little. Exclusively. I love you, and I'm really sorry Kelly. I honestly didn't mean for any of this to happen," Olivia explained. My resolve weakened. I didn't even know what to do at this point. The tears filled my eyes, and I turned away before an ugly sob left my chest. This was what I was dreading. Why did everyone leave me? Why? Was I some kind of monster?

"Oh my God, Kels. Please don't cry," Olivia said, and I felt like slapping her at that moment.

"Olivia, if you really don't want to go meet your Daddy"– I sneered the word– "with a black eye, then you'll refrain from speaking to me," I growled.

"Kels, please, I was just kidding. I wanted this to be a surprise. James asked both of us to move in with him. You know I love you too much to do something like that to you. Please forgive me. I admit it was a joke in bad taste," Olivia said, realizing the pain she had just caused me. When I heard those words, I turned to Olivia with a murderous expression of my face.

"I've never been so scared before in my life. Please don't repeat that," I said coldly then walked out of the room. I went to the bedroom, cried a little then went back to the bathroom. Olivia was sitting there with a dejected look on her face. I sighed when I saw her.

"You're forgiven. Stop looking like a puppy that was run over," I said, rolling my eyes. Olivia woke up suddenly and launched herself at me.

"Thank you, Kels. I don't know what I was thinking with your past and all. I was just trying to be... I just wanted to play a prank on you," she explained, and she looked so sad that I rolled my eyes and hugged her.

"It's okay. Just don't repeat it," I said, and she nodded frantically. Then she placed a small kiss on my lips and walked away. I took another bag and joined her to start packing.

"When did James have the time to tell you all this?" I was curious because I knew that he got out of work even later than me sometimes.

"He came home and met me. He told me he was going to finalize some things. I don't know what, though," she said, and I let out a small mhmm. I continued packing. Then we moved to the living room. Looking at everything was overwhelming. Daddy's house was already completely furnished, so I didn't know what we were going to do with all this. Unless we like rented a storage unit and the rent of those things didn't come for cheap.

"Daddy said we should leave everything else. He'd take care of it," Olivia supplied helpfully when she saw me looking at everything.

"Oh, okay," I said. I left. I was feeling kinda jealous at that moment. But I knew that once I had decided to share, I had taken the consequences as well. I couldn't leave the relationship though because of some petty jealousy. I was just going to spend five to ten minutes alone to clear my head. It always worked. And it did this time. I got out of the bedroom, where I had been moping a little. Olivia was standing there, a worried look on her face.

"Are you okay?" she asked.

"Yes, babes. I'm sorry sometimes I just have to remind myself that neither of you is going to betray me. I get in my feelings sometimes. I'm sorry," I said with a sigh.

"Hey, no need to apologize. Honestly, you're very strong. You welcomed me into your home, and you welcomed me into your Daddy's arms. I love just how strong you are because, to be honest with you. I'm not sure that I would have done same. I am so proud of you," Olivia explained. I teared up and took Olivia into my arms. We stayed there for quite a long time. That was how Daddy found us.

"My two princesses," he said, and we let go

of each other. Both of us jumped and ran towards him.

"Daddy I missed you so much," I said as he hugged us right to him.

"I missed you too little one," Daddy said, and I smiled.

"Are you done packing?" he asked, and both of us hopelessly shook our heads.

"Have you packed the essentials, though?" he asked.

"Yes, Daddy," Olivia answered since I had barely had time to pack anything.

"Good. I will get the bags, and we will finish packing all this tomorrow. Because I guess we're all tired."

"Okay, Daddy. Thank you, Daddy. You're the best Daddy ever," I said and kissed his cheek. We showed Daddy where the bags were, and he took them out to his car. Then buckled us into the car, and we drove off to his place. It was a quick ride as there wasn't a lot of traffic.

"Welcome home, princess. Welcome home,

cupcake," Daddy said as soon as we got into the house.

***

It was time to lay down everything. We were sitting in the living room, Olivia and I next to each other. We were waiting for Daddy to say something.

"Okay, so I have destroyed the other contract. Both of you will read this one and if you are displeased with anything. If you're not, though, you can sign right away," James said. He gave both of us the contracts. The title was OUR DDLG RELATIONSHIP: JAMES, KELLY, AND OLIVIA. I liked my name was first. I started reading through and nodding my head as I agreed with everything that James had written. He had asked us what type of things we would like in the contract before he wrote it up, I liked that he did stuff like that. The only thing that had my concerned was the fact that Daddy had added one rule about smoking. I was worried that Olivia would not be able to quit just because he told her to. I asked Daddy for a pen and signed. A while after, Olivia signed as well. When she did, we looked at each other and squealed. Then we hugged each other. We were officially littles to our Daddy.

Chapter 12

Olivia's POV

Today was great. And it was going to keep being awesome. I had come back from work early. And what James had told me when I got back home had put me in an instant good mood. Firstly, all three of us were going to go out and get dinner. Then we were going to do a scene at the kink club. I didn't know why, but Daddy had said this scene was going to be special, and I believed him. He was my Daddy, after all. We waited for Kelly to get back from work. Honestly, I didn't know what I would have done without her in my life. I would probably be stranded somewhere, lost, alone, and lonely. But because of her, I had a Daddy now. And every day, I was loving her more and more, and not just as a friend. When she came back, I relayed the news to her. Daddy gave us an hour to get ready for dinner. And his exact words were, "Even if you're not ready in an hour, I'm dragging you out, naked or clothed."

An hour wasn't a lot, but we could do something with it. Both of us showered. Then we proceeded to get ready. Yes. We were littles. But that didn't mean that we weren't in touch with our femininity. We started with our hair. While I did big curls, Kelly straightened hers. Then we moved on to makeup. We kept it quite simple, the only extra thing being the lipstick we put on. Then we put our dresses and shoes on, and we were good to go.

We went to a fancy restaurant. It was like Daddy was celebrating something, but he didn't want to let us in on the joke. We were left wondering. And we didn't have a lot of options because right after dinner, we had a scene. I hadn't been in a public scene for about a year now. And I honestly couldn't wait. It was something I enjoyed doing. It made me let go of my inhibitions. And it took all my stress away. I felt so free when I was doing a scene. It was liberating. Soon enough, we were done with dinner. Daddy drove us to the club. We stood around for a while with the other littles. They knew now that we shared a Daddy, and it was good that all of them were open-minded because none of them judged.

"Honestly, if I had the chance to share him with you guys, I would take it," one of our friends said.

"Don't tell my Daddy I said that though," she added sheepishly, and we laughed. From the way they were talking, I knew just how lucky I was to have a friend and lover like Kelly. She was so selfless. She had agreed to share her Daddy with me. And it baffled me every single time that I looked at James. It made me realize just how much I loved her.

"Did Daddy tell you we'll have a scene tonight?" I asked her sipping at the juice in my class. These clothes were restricting. I wanted to be naked or in a diaper. Not in the skin tight red dress I had decided to wear. I noticed Kelly fidgeting as well, and I concluded that she had the same problem.

"Yes, and he made it sound so ominous. Maybe it's because it's his first scene," she said.

"Maybe," was my only reply.

"Go get ready for the scene," Daddy whispered to us. I shivered at his voice and obeyed him. I couldn't wait. I couldn't wait to be completely possessed by him.

James's POV

Handcuffs. I had handcuffed both of them. I felt in control. They couldn't do anything. Black blindfolds. Just enough to keep them from knowing exactly what I wanted to do. I wanted them to anticipate every move I was going to make. Every kiss I was going to place on their bodies. Every touch I was going to trace into their skin. I wanted to keep them from seeing me lick my lips at their beautiful bodies and seductive postures. I didn't want them to see me walk towards them. But I didn't want their senses numb. I wanted them to feel my presence behind them. I wanted them to feel my breath as I traced it across their earlobes. I wanted them to shiver when I gently traced their backs with my finger. I wanted them to feel me touch their sides, run my hands along their hips, and trace it right up to their soft breasts, barely touching them. I wanted them to feel me. I wanted them to know just who their Daddy was.

I started by tugging on their shirts. Every movement I made to one, I made to the other. It was dark, but I could tell who was who. I just didn't want to let it matter at this moment. All that counted right now was me touching them and giving them pleasure. I knew that they couldn't take off their shirts alone. And even if they could, their hands were cuffed. So I tugged on the shirt made a hole. I repeated the same process with the next person. Then I tugged at those holes. I pulled until their gorgeous black bra just barely covered the skin on their chests. I kissed their necks, making sure to alternate and whisper some exciting thing into their ears. Then I moved my lips up to their mouths and kissed them, one after the other, passionately. Their moans made me almost lose control. I wanted much more.

Oh, God. Did I want more? I wanted so much more of them than there was revealed. They looked so sexy there. Vulnerable. The excitement in their bodies. From their quivering thighs to their shaky breaths. They were scared. Not scared of me. They were scared of the unknown. But it was obvious that they wanted this. They wanted more. Their little moans and tight nipples gave them away. They didn't know what I was going to do next. And that made them even more excited. And it made them feel powerful yet so powerless at the same time. Slowly, and teasingly I moved my hand down to their underwear and rubbed at their princess parts. I was standing in the middle, where I could easily touch them both, as much as I wanted to. I knew they weren't ready yet for me to touch their wet, quivering pussy lips. But I did. And I rubbed until I had them moaning. Oh, God, the sound of their moans together. It was like I was listening to the sweetest music.

One of them moaned again before I put my hand inside their panties. I slowly slipped a finger inside her. Felt how bad they were clenching against me. Almost as if they were in sync, both of them moaned very loudly. I alternated kisses on their backs, making them moan even more. I knew that they were close to cumming. Even though I had barely done anything yet.

"Don't cum yet, baby girl," I said, moving my fingers in and out of both of rhythmically. I knew it excited both of them that they didn't know who exactly I was talking to.

"Don't. Not yet." One of them moaned and squirmed around, trying so hard not to.

"You look so sexy, trying not to cum." She moaned as I added another finger and moved faster. I felt her pulse and felt her quiver. Both of them were so close. But I didn't want them to cum yet. I had more interesting things to do to them. I removed my fingers completely, ignoring their moans of protest. One after the other, I removed their panties completely, making sure to drop little slaps on their wet pussies. Then I bent and licked her soaking princess parts, and repeated the same thing with the other.

"Don't you fucking cum yet..." I said quietly.

"Daddy...please..." Kelly whispered. She was more sensitive.

"No." I licked both of them more and more. Tasting their delicious wet parts. I pushed my tongue completely into each of them alternatively, and Olivia screamed.

"You can cum now, baby girl." She sighed, gasped and screamed, and came all over. Then as if in tempo, Kelly let out a loud scream as well and came. I didn't uncuff them. And I didn't remove the blindfolds. I took one of the collars, went to Kelly, put it around her neck and locked it. "I love you, baby girl," I whispered and placed a small kiss on her mouth. I walked the other way to Olivia with the other collar, did the same as I had done for Kelly, then placed a kiss on her lips as well.

"I love you cupcake." After doing that, I removed the blindfolds and handcuffs. The scene was officially over.

Chapter 13

Kelly's POV

Daddy had collared us. He had collared us! The scene was the most beautiful one of my entire existence, and I wasn't sure that anything else could top it. Being collared was serious. It was basically marriage. It was telling us just how serious he was about us. I loved him so much. I didn't know how I could show him. But I loved him so much. Olivia and I went out to get him a gift to show him just how much we loved him. And we also wanted our mark on him. Call it being possessive. We didn't care. No other person was going to look at our man.

"Do you think he'd like this?" Olivia asked, lifting up a bracelet. We were at a jewelry store trying to find something for him, and it was turning out to be kind of a struggle.

"He would never even be able to wear it. He would have to remove it at the hospital," I said, sighing. It was hard buying a gift for a doctor when the job was so practical. Olivia sighed. I sighed again. Then a brilliant idea crossed my mind.

"Why don't we get him a chain. A beautiful silver chain, maybe?" I asked, looking at Olivia for her input. She was smiling.

"That's a great idea. And then we add two rings to it because he's ours. And no one will ever approach him!" she exclaimed, and I laughed.

"That's a great idea," I replied. We started looking for the items. Olivia was looking for the rings while I was looking for the chain. I found something. It was simple, and it honestly screamed James

"Daddy will like it," Olivia said when I showed her. She had gotten two beautiful silver rings. After paying, we left the shop and went back home.

Daddy was already home when we got there, which was a huge surprise. We looked at each other because normally he was home way later than all this. So we didn't really understand what he was doing home.

"Hi Daddy," I said, placing a kiss on his cheek. Olivia did the same thing, and he smiled at both of us. I loved seeing Daddy smile. I exchanged a look with Olivia, and she nodded. Since I was the one who had the package in my hand, I was the one who was going to do the honours.

"Daddy, we got something for you," I said.

"What would that be, Princess?" he asked, and I removed it from the little bag I was holding.

"Open it," I encouraged with a smile. Daddy looked at weirdly because it was a ring box. I'm pretty sure he had completely misunderstood. I fought the urge to laugh. Daddy opened the gift, and the expression on his face turned serious. He stared at the gift for a while then looked up at us.

"I love you too. Come here and hug me." I rushed forward and hugged him then made room for Olivia to do same.

"So, you have something to tell us? Why are you home so early?" I asked, settling myself in his lap while Olivia helped him put the necklace on.

"We are going on a trip. We are going to the Bahamas," he said, and Olivia and I looked at each other and squealed.

"Oh my God, Daddy. You're the best," she squealed, then kissed him on the mouth. I watched them as Daddy deepened the kiss, and I shifted a bit in his lap. Now was not the time to get aroused.

"When are we leaving?" I asked. I was asking all the questions because Olivia was being very, very horny, and couldn't keep her hands off Daddy.

"In about thirty minutes. So you better go pack." We stood and ran to the nursery excitedly. This was going to be fun.

***

Once again, like the first time Daddy and I went on

vacation, we had use his friend's private plane. I had to admit that it was way more convenient than commercial flights. And faster. But I had never been to the Bahamas, so I didn't know about that, to be honest. The place was even more beautiful than in the pictures. Daddy had gotten us a house that had its own private beach, just like in Hawaii. It was great because that way, we were free to do whatever we wanted without people staring at us like we were weirdos.

"Go change. Let's go to the beach," Daddy said. I changed into a baby pink bikini. I hoped it would remind Daddy of the first night we were together. Then Olivia changed into a sexy one piece that had no fabric on the sides, exposing her tiny waist. We were good to go. Daddy was in swim trunks, and he looked edible. But now was not the time for such thoughts. We had to go enjoy our time on the beach.

"Kelly, you remember last time. When I call you, you listen," he said, and I nodded.

"Yes, Daddy," I said and pretended to salute

him as Olivia, and I headed down towards the sea.

"What happened last time?" Olivia asked.

"Well, I almost got drowned," I explained, and she widened her eyes.

"Damn babes. Thank goodness you're okay," she said, and I hugged her. I loved this girl. We started splashing each other with water. It was fun. We kept on laughing and giggling. Then we took it up a notch. I'd splash her, then I'd touch her crotch a little a giggle. She'd do same to me and rub my nipple. We kept on doing that until Daddy called. We turned and looked, but he was coming our way.

"Why don't you include me in that?" James asked. Olivia and I smiled, and each of us started splashing him with water, without giving him the chance to get a hold of us. We were having so much fun, then he caught me.

"I've caught you now," he said creepily, and I shrieked.

"Daddy!!" We laughed and then all of a sudden, he kissed me. He opens his mouth slightly, inviting me to deepen the kiss. He tastes like the island around us; the tang of brine and the sweetness of fruit. Warmth radiates from his body, enveloping me, protecting me. I circle my hands up his neck, tangling them in the long locks of soft hair. He pulls his lips away from my own, breaking the kiss. My eyes snap open in protest but close in pleasure once again when he begins trailing kisses along my jawbone, pausing to suckle at the soft corners of my ear. I trace the curve of his spine, reveling in the coils of muscle beneath my fingertips. I stop when I reach his hips, which are so agonizingly close to my own. I reach beneath him to untie the drawstring on his shorts, but quick hands stop me.

"Not yet," he whispers in my ear, warm breath tickling the wisps of hair around it. He grabs my wrists, one in each hand, and brings them up above my head. I stare at him in confusion, but my inquiring gaze is only met with a mischievous grin. He trails his hands lightly down my arms, fingertips just barely making contact, down to my waist, before circling back up to the curve of my breasts. He traces them lightly over my bikini, the brief contact sending my nipples to attention. Deft hands untie the knots behind my back and around my neck, allowing him to pull away the thin material in a single sweeping motion. The cool air on my naked breasts releases a sigh of contentment from me; I have never had them exposed outside. He cups my right breast in one hand, massaging the nipple with his thumb, while his tongue teases my left; he flicks and circles it with his tongue, and I moan, unable to repress the pang of pleasure the motion is sending down my navel. I hook one leg around his waist, raising my hip to meet him. A low moan grumbles in his throat, and he firmly pushes me down again; he lifts his eyes to mine as he slides down my body, kissing my belly, moving lower and lower.

"I said not yet," he whispers, pulling away my bikini bottoms with nimble fingers. At this point, Olivia straddles my face and lowers her dripping wetness unto my mouth. I start lapping it up, making sure to nip at her clit a little. Daddy buries his face between my thighs, sucking, and licking, skilfully flicking his tongue over my pearl. I arch my back in ecstasy, moaning as waves of pleasure roll over my body. I grasp my breast with one hand, digging into the flesh, while the other runs through his hair. He's moaning, and It's almost enough to send me over the edge. With Olivia still riding my face, Daddy guides himself into me, slowly at first, the tip of his cock just barely teasing my entrance, before filling my core with a rough groan of relief that tells me he wants this as much as I do. He rocks his hips into mine, gently, and steadily. Then faster, and harder, his breath mingling with mine, gasping, moaning, a mixture of pain and pleasure. Our arms and legs are entwined.

I moan into Olivia's wetness, holding her legs up as Daddy continues pounding me with an urgency that reverberates through my bones. The heat between my thighs builds and builds until I can't take it any longer; my body tenses and shudders, a shiver running down my spine as my body collapses into a pool of gratification. His muscles tensed tightly, not long after, groaning loudly as he spills his cum deep within me. We, me, him, Olivia, crumble together in the sand, still entwined, slick with sweat. Faces close together. I can feel him smiling behind my closed eyes, a tightening of his grasp on me as his breath falls into the steady rhythm of sleep. The crash of waves on the shoreline is the last thing I hear before joining him in slumber.

When I woke up I was back in the beautiful hotel room lying on the king-size bed in the middle of the bedroom. James had really outdone himself with this vacation. I could hear Olivia playing in the living room and James on the balcony talking on the phone. I stayed in bed, listening to the waves crash on the shore and sighed in contented bliss.

"Daddy," I called as I yawned and stretched after hearing him end his phone call. Suddenly, I was greeted by the sight of James, only wearing a towel around his hips. He ran his fingers through his hair and smiled at me.

"Hey baby girl. You had a big sleep. Ready to have a bath and then join Oli playing in the living room. She has been building a big tower that I'm sure she will let you help make," James said as he came over to me and picked me up in his arms. I loved how strong he was and snuggled into him as he carried me to the bathroom.

Placing me down in the bath, he ran warm water over my sleepy body and washed me clean before drying me off with one of the fluffy white hotel towels and wrapping me in one of the bathrobes.

"Such a pretty girl," James said as he led me back to the bedroom. He placed me on the floor and opened my bathrobe. Sliding a diaper under my hips as I quietly obeyed his gentle taps to move me this way and that. I liked that he knew that it took me a while before I was able to come out of my sleepy state. He powdered me and fastened the diaper around my waist before placing me in one of the onesies he had packed for me. It was pink with clouds on it, and I loved how he always knew which one I wanted to wear.

After he had finished dressing me, he put my paci in my mouth and watched as I made a beeline for the living room. I had not forgotten that James had said Olivia was building a block tower, and I was very interested in being part of that process.

I crawled along the carpeted floor to the living room and sat next to Olivia. She threw her arms around me and held me tight, pulling me into her lap and continuing to play. Her little age was older than mine, and she liked being bigger than me. I didn't mind, it was nice to be the baby. Everything was perfect, and life was only just getting started.

Who is Tina Moore?

Tina Moore has enjoyed the lifestyle of a Mommy Domme for several years. She began exploring kink and BDSM in her youth and found her love of being a strict Mommy Domme in early 2000. Tina Moore is now an author of many MDLG, DDLG and ABDL themed novels.

Follow her on:

Author Page on Amazon

Instagram @tinamoore.kdp